THE QUEEN'S ADVANTAGE

ALSO BY JESSIE MIHALIK

The Rogue Queen Series

The Queen's Gambit

The Queen's Advantage

The Consortium Rebellion Series

Polaris Rising

Aurora Blazing

Chaos Reigning

THE QUEEN'S ADVANTAGE

JESSIE MIHALIK

THE QUEEN'S ADVANTAGE
Copyright © 2019 by Jessie Mihalik
Ebook ISBN-13: 9781641970891
Print ISBN-13: 9781075962097
IS Print ISBN: 9781641971447
Excerpt from *Aurora Blazing* copyright © by Jessie Mihalik

NYLA Publishing
121 W 27th St., Suite 1201, New York, NY 10001
http://www.nyliterary.com

To Dustin, my love.
We have the best adventures.
Here's to many more.

ACKNOWLEDGMENTS

I'd like to thank the following people for their help and support.

Thanks to my awesome agent, Sarah E. Younger, who whipped this story into shape. I may have grumbled about edits, but the story is far, far better now. And thank you to Natanya Wheeler and everyone at NYLA who helped bring the book into the world!

Thanks to Patrick Ferguson and Tracy Smith for reading early chapters and offering feedback. Thank you to Whitney Bates for agreeing to cowork at weird hours when we're both available. And thank you all for your patience when I disappear into the writing cave.

My deepest gratitude to the beta readers who generously volunteered their time and energy to improve the story: Regina Brandt, Chi-An Chien, and Kelly Loudamy. Your insightful feedback made the story so much better. Thank you so much!

My love and appreciation to my husband, Dustin, who is always my very first reader and biggest supporter. I love you!

Finally, thanks to all of the readers who followed along as the story was posted on my website, www.jessiemihalik.com. I am planning to continue the series in the late fall of 2019, and once again it will be posted first as a free serial.

1

Butterflies fluttered in my stomach as I secured the last of my supplies in *Invictia*'s cargo bay. Now I had everything I needed for my trip to Koan, the Kos Empire's capital city. In just a few hours, I would get to see Emperor Valentin Kos in person for the first time in over a month.

Unfortunately, this trip was more business than pleasure. I'd promised Valentin four weeks of my time to help him root out the traitors in his court, and I'd done all of the remote research I could, so now it was time to meet his advisors in person. I was sure they were going to be delighted to welcome the Rogue Queen into their midst—the Rogue Queen who had tricked them out of several million credits.

Ha.

Arietta Mueller, my best friend and head of security, grumbled under her breath from her position near *Invictia*'s cargo bay door. She worried about me like it was her job—and it kind of was. Tall, with blond hair and pale skin, Ari was gorgeous. She was impossible to ignore even when she wasn't audibly calling attention to herself.

I had decided not to take Ari with me on this trip, but she was still trying to change my mind. She had waged her campaign for the last two weeks with the ruthless determination that made her a terror on the battlefield. She'd even gotten her wife involved, and Dr. Stella Mueller had long ago perfected her intimidation tactics.

Despite everything, I'd held firm. I was going to be gone for at least two weeks, maybe longer. I'd planned to split my four-week debt into two trips, but if things went exceedingly well—or poorly—this trip, then I might need to stay the whole month. I needed Ari and Stella here in Arx to keep an eye on things. I had other advisors, but none I trusted as much as my closest friends.

Cargo secure, I joined Ari near the door. "Spit it out," I said.

"What?"

"You've been grumbling more than usual for the last ten minutes. What's up? Are you concerned about Imogen?" I asked, naming the guard I was taking with me. I could generally protect myself, but I'd decided a second set of eyes in hostile territory might be a good idea. "I thought she was your first choice."

"*I* should be going with you, Samara."

I took a deep breath and tried to remember that I would be just as annoying if our roles were reversed.

She continued, "I can't shake the feeling that something is going to go wrong. Valentin's advisors tried to kill him and you're putting yourself right in the middle of it. It's making me crazy. I'm sorry, I know I'm being a pain in the ass."

"I'm uneasy, too," I confessed. In order to help Valentin ferret out who was loyal and who wasn't, I would be inserting myself directly into the web of lies and treachery binding him and his court. I'd spent weeks carefully researching his top advisors, and while I hadn't uncovered anything definitively treasonous, several of them had some questionable connections. "That's why I want

2

you here to look after things for the Rogue Coalition. You know I can take care of myself."

She nodded in grumpy agreement. "I know. And I made Imogen promise to stick to you like glue, but I still don't like it."

"You don't have to like it—"

"I just have to do it," she finished. "Yeah, yeah, I know. Come say good-bye to Stella, then get out of here before I change my mind and lock you in your suite." Concern lurked under her gruff words.

"I'll be careful, Ari," I promised.

"You'd better be," Stella demanded as she climbed the cargo ramp. "I won't be there to patch you up this time." Stella was a few centimeters taller than me, with warm brown skin, long dark hair, and dark eyes that sparkled with hidden humor. She was as beautiful as her wife, and they made a stunning couple.

At thirty, I was old enough to be secure about my own appearance. My face was attractive enough, but I would never be mistaken for beautiful. However, my petite build, light brown skin, and long dark hair gave me a delicate charm. I wasn't in the same league as Ari and Stella, and that worked well for me. It was harder to blend in when every eye in the room was drawn to you.

"I'm hoping I won't need to be patched up this time," I said, "but if I do, you know I'll miss your gentle bedside manner."

Stella huffed out a laugh. She was one of the best doctors I knew, but she ran medical like a despot. "I'll remember that the next time you come to me with your insides on the outside."

I grinned at her. "You know I love you, Stella. Try to keep Ari from sulking too much while I'm gone."

"I could break you in half and then you wouldn't have to go," Ari threatened mildly.

Stella rolled her eyes. "Return to us in one piece because stars know that none of the rest of us can hold this ship together."

"Nor do we want to," Ari added, "so be careful."

"I will be," I promised. I just hoped it was a promise I could keep.

INVICTIA TUNNELED TO ACHENSTEV PRIME, the Kos Empire's planetary headquarters, in a single transit. We were practically neighbors, cosmically speaking. The planet glowed lush green and sparkling blue on *Invictia*'s screens. Koan was situated near the equator and offered a temperate climate year-round.

We were awaiting landing clearance and had been parked in orbit for nearly fifteen minutes while a corvette-class warship slowly closed on us. Imogen growled when ground control put us off again. "Maybe they're hoping we die of old age before they have to let us land," she said. "Or maybe they're waiting for that corvette to get within attack range and solve the problem for them."

I kept a wary eye on the corvette's trajectory. Valentin knew I was coming. I wouldn't expect his warships to be a threat, but someone in his cabinet also wanted him dead, so perhaps the treachery ran deeper than I thought.

I kept my thoughts to myself and my tone light. "Maybe it just takes time to roll out the appropriate pomp and circumstance for a visiting queen. I'm very important, you know." I tilted my chin in the air and waved an imperious arm.

Imogen snorted, then laughed. "If it were up to you, we'd sneak in a back door."

Truth be told, I'd suggested it, but Ari had forbidden me from trying it in no uncertain terms. This was to be an official visit where the Kos Empire *should* be obliged to ensure my safety, but current circumstances were testing that theory. I wasn't worried about Valentin stabbing me in the back, but I wouldn't trust his advisors not to try, given half an opportunity.

As it was, I decided I'd waited long enough. Patience had never been my strong suit, and in another three minutes, the corvette would be close enough to be a real threat. I reached out to Valentin via a voice-only neural link. When he accepted the connection, I asked, *Are your ground crews planning to let us land sometime today or am I going to have to cause an intergalactic incident?*

I could hear the smile in his mental voice when he said, *Maybe save the incident for later. I'll contact the ground crews and get you clearance, then meet you at the spaceport.*

He closed the connection before I could tell him that he didn't need to meet me in person. Nervous anticipation rippled through my system. I'd be seeing Valentin face-to-face, and soon.

"Finally," Imogen muttered under her breath when the approval came through a minute later.

"I linked Valentin," I said. "He's meeting us at the spaceport."

Imogen slanted me a sly glance, but she kept her thoughts to herself. Despite living in Arx for nearly two years, she still tended to think of me as queen first, Samara second, and acted accordingly. I hoped this trip would break through some of her reserve.

Invictia cut smoothly through the atmosphere. She'd spent weeks in dry dock for repairs after my last run-in with a warship. There were still a few things that needed fixing, but she was space-worthy, and there was no other ship I'd rather have. *Invictia* had been my first real home, and she'd gotten me out of more scrapes than I could count. This ship was not only my most valuable possession, she was also my most cherished.

It was a relief to be landing rather than trying to outrun a corvette.

As we approached, Koan sparkled below us, a metropolis of glass and metal reaching for the sky. The Imperial Garden—a huge, three-hundred-hectare park that surrounded the palace—looked like a green oasis in the heart of the city.

The palace itself was a sprawling complex. A large, ornate stone building housed the main residence and ceremonial chambers. While the building was in pristine condition, it clearly was a product of another era—one long past—and a testament to the lasting power of the Kos Empire. A few other buildings clustered nearby, including a tall modern glass tower that held most of the government offices and guest quarters.

I'd been to Koan once, many years ago, and the memories were not happy ones. I hoped this trip would end far better.

Valentin had gotten us cleared to land in the palace spaceport at the edge of the park, which meant I had to have my game face on as soon as we touched down. I would've *much* preferred landing in the main spaceport outside the city and making my own way to the palace, but that wasn't how queens traveled. *Unfortunately.*

Invictia settled onto an outdoor landing pad, between two larger ships painted in the black and red of the Kos Empire colors. The vid screens showed a small group of people piling out of a quartet of transports. Everyone was dressed in full ceremonial attire.

I was glad Ari and Stella had talked me into buying a new wardrobe. I didn't care how I looked, but based on the cluster of people below, Stella had been right—no one would take me seriously in my usual clothes. Here, I was Queen Rani of the Rogue Coalition, not Samara Rani, a nobody from a backwater planet no one had ever heard of. And while it might be fun to see his advisors turn their noses up at me, I was here to help Valentin, not stir up trouble.

At least not yet.

I stood and brushed a hand down my black blouse and gray

slacks. I'd had my new clothes custom-tailored in technical fabrics that were hideously expensive. The fabric looked like a normal weave, but it could block light blades and glancing plasma pulses, so the expense had been worth it.

The tailor had also added an assortment of hidden pockets for my weapons, even to the dresses, so anyone who thought to catch me unarmed would be in for a surprise.

My feet were encased in a pair of black ankle boots with short, sturdy heels because I'd drawn the line at shoes I couldn't run in. I'd also brought a range of flats and a pair of tall boots.

"Ready?" I asked.

Imogen nodded and stood. At a meter seventy-five, she was ten centimeters taller than me. She wore slim black pants and a pale pink button-down that complemented her deep brown skin. Short, tight black curls haloed her head and accented her impressive cheekbones. Together with her curvy, hourglass figure, she looked beautiful and harmless.

It was exactly the right look for a bodyguard.

Her appearance didn't reveal that she had speed and strength augments that rivaled my own. She could lift and carry a man twice her size without breaking a sweat. And if it came down to it, she could put him on the ground in half a heartbeat. I'd seen her in training and would not want to go hand-to-hand with her on my best day.

We stopped in the cargo hold. I lifted the hem of my blouse, revealing the holster tucked into the curve of my waist. An undershirt prevented it from chafing—this wasn't my first rodeo. I slipped a small plasma pistol into the holster and dropped the hem. The flowing fabric of my blouse concealed both gun and holster.

Imogen didn't need to be quite so subtle. She slung a utility belt around her waist and holstered a much larger plasma pistol.

We'd debated putting her in full combat armor, but had decided it would send the wrong message. I'd desperately wanted to watch Valentin's advisors' expressions when they figured out my bodyguard came kitted out in prototype Kos armor, but I'd managed to refrain. Barely.

Between the two of us, we had three trunks of clothes and accessories. Most of that space was dedicated to my new wardrobe. A fourth trunk held all of the weapons and other gadgets we might need. It would stay on the ship until I was sure we could smuggle it in without getting searched.

I linked to the sled that held the three trunks we were taking and put it in follow mode. It hovered at knee height. I nudged it to ensure the gyroscopes were working. It slid back a few centimeters, then stabilized. Good enough.

"Don't let them separate us," Imogen reminded me. "We should be put in a suite together. If we are not, then you should insist on it."

"I will. If I miss something, speak up. I'm not used to having a bodyguard. I'll likely forget some of the rules, so let me know when that happens. I won't get mad at you for speaking your mind."

Imogen smiled. "I'll remind you that you said that. Ari warned me to keep an eye on you or you'd vanish, so expect me to be constantly underfoot."

"Ari worries too much, but I'll try not to vanish without letting you know."

I opened the cargo bay door. Valentin stood at the bottom of the ramp, clad in a formal red coat, black pants, and tall black boots. Black braided rope encircled one shoulder and the host of medals on his chest must've weighed a kilogram, at least. A brilliant gold crown sparkled against his dark hair.

I smiled despite myself. How he managed to remain incredibly handsome even in that ridiculous getup, I'd never know, but he did. Stella had tried to persuade me that I should wear a crown and I'd laughed. If she found out that Valentin had arrived in full regalia, I'd never hear the end of it.

Valentin grinned at me and the swarm of butterflies in my stomach turned into a herd of elephants.

I led Imogen and the cargo sled toward Valentin. Once we were clear of the cargo bay, I used my mental link to *Invictia* to put the ship into lockdown with a two-meter proximity alert that would alert me if anyone approached the ship. *Invictia* wouldn't unlock for anyone other than myself or Imogen, but I wanted to know if anyone was poking around where they shouldn't be.

I tore my eyes away from Valentin long enough to assess the people with him. Luka Fox, Valentin's bodyguard, was clad in all black and towered behind Valentin's right shoulder. Luka had wavy ice-blond hair, a muscular build, and a scowl that would send lesser mortals fleeing for their lives.

When he caught my eye, his scowl deepened. I'd met him in Arx, and I was not his favorite person, mostly because I'd let Ari commandeer his armor. I smiled brightly at him. His eyes narrowed, but otherwise, he didn't rise to my baiting.

To Valentin's left and a meter behind him, three men and three women waited in long black and red ceremonial robes. These were Valentin's top advisors. I'd researched them, and I was pleased to find that I recognized all of their faces. One or more of them wanted Valentin dead.

My job was to figure out who.

The advisors' expressions ranged from open hostility to fake, plastic smiles. Only one person seemed to be genuinely happy to be here—Myra Shah, the Imperial Guard advisor. She was the only one who acknowledged me with a slight incline of her head. The others stared through me as if I didn't exist.

Valentin closed the distance between us, took my hands, and kissed the air next to my cheek. Heat rushed through me as I remembered the last time we were this close, but he kept the greeting formal. "Welcome to Koan, Queen Rani," he said, his voice warm. "The Kos Empire will do our utmost to ensure your comfort and safety during your stay."

He let go and stepped back. The medals on his chest jingled every time he moved. It grounded me in the moment, and I was grateful. He shifted and the medals clinked together again. I bit my lip to prevent myself from snickering at him. From the laughter in his gray eyes, he knew exactly what I was thinking.

I bowed a few degrees—enough to be respectful, but so not much that I appeared subservient. Stella had coached me on the proper etiquette. "The Rogue Coalition thanks you for your hospitality, Emperor Kos," I said. "I am here on a peaceful diplomatic mission."

Someone in the group snorted.

I leaned around Valentin and pointedly stared at his advisors. "I may be here for peace, but I am well-equipped to defend myself, should it be necessary." I gave them a cold smile. "Try me and you will regret it."

2

Chaos erupted behind Valentin. "You dare—" Oskar Krystopa, the dark-haired military strategy advisor started, but Valentin slashed a hand through the air, and Oskar bit off the rest of the sentence.

"Your safety will be our priority," Valentin said. "Allow me to introduce my bodyguard and advisors."

"Of course," I agreed with a smile as fake as the welcome I had received from said advisors. I had to pretend that I didn't already know far more about each of them than they would probably prefer.

Valentin swept an arm toward Luka. "You've already met Luka Fox, my bodyguard. If your guard needs anything while you are here, Luka will take care of it."

I nodded at Luka. I wasn't an expert in imperial etiquette, but I was pretty sure Valentin had snubbed his advisors by introducing his bodyguard first—a snub I was happy to continue.

"This is Imogen Weber, my bodyguard," I said. "Imogen, meet Emperor Kos and Luka Fox."

"A pleasure," Imogen said with a short bow. After a brief glance at Valentin, her eyes returned to Luka before scanning the area. She always kept Luka in sight, and she had the loose, ready body posture that meant she saw him as a threat. Luka's expression remained impossible to read, but he watched Imogen with steady focus.

Valentin turned to Oskar, who still seethed over my very reasonable statement. "This is Oskar Krystopa. He leads military strategy."

Oskar was older, probably in his mid-fifties, despite the lack of gray in his black hair. He had olive skin, green eyes, and curls that just brushed the tops of his ears. He would've been handsome if he hadn't been so busy scowling, but based on the lines in his forehead—and the rumor mill—this was his perpetual expression. He did not bow, and he managed to make his tone convey his sneer. "Queen Rani."

I gave him a bright, sharp smile. "Advisor Krystopa."

Next, Valentin introduced Junior Mobb, the medical advisor and chief doctor. A handsome man in his thirties with ebony skin and close-cropped black hair, Junior appeared indifferent to my presence. His curt greeting seemed less like rudeness and more like distraction. He had the distant look of someone conversing via neural link. He was, by all accounts, a brilliant doctor.

Hannah Perkins was introduced as the head of diplomatic relations. She was a faded beauty with wrinkled ivory skin and graying red hair, but her eyes were sharp. She wasn't as openly hostile as Oskar, but she wasn't welcoming, either. She was married to Valentin's distant cousin and had been an advisor for nearly thirty years.

Asmo Copley, the advisor for domestic affairs, immediately rubbed me the wrong way. Tan skin, dark brown hair, and brown eyes were common enough, but he'd been blessed with exceeding beauty—and he knew it. He laid on the false charm with a shovel.

I smiled politely and ignored him. He came from a powerful family and expected me to fall at his feet. When I didn't, I became a challenge, someone interesting. Before he could try a new tactic, Valentin moved on.

Joanna Cook, the science and technology advisor and lead scientist, was a no-nonsense pale blonde woman in her forties who looked like she'd rather be anywhere else than standing in the open, in a formal robe, greeting royalty. She wore glasses despite the fact that a myriad of options existed to fix her vision, either with surgery or augmentation. According to my research, she was smart and driven, but mostly kept to herself.

Valentin turned to the final woman, the only person who had acknowledged me on my way from the ship. "And last, but by no means least, Myra Shah, head of the Imperial Guard." Warmth infused his voice, a first.

Myra was around my age with golden skin and a chin-length straight black bob. Her face was more striking than beautiful, all sharp angles and slashing eyebrows, but her expression appeared genuinely welcoming and her dark eyes sparkled with intelligence. "Queen Rani," she said with a shallow bow, "it is a pleasure to finally meet you. Welcome to Koan."

I returned her bow. "Thank you, Advisor Shah. The pleasure is mine." And this time, I almost meant it. I hadn't been able to turn up anything questionable in my research on her—and I had tried. As part of the Imperial Guard, she had the best access to Valentin, so she was the biggest threat if she turned traitor.

She grinned knowingly. "Please, call me Myra, and let me know if you need anything during your stay."

I inclined my head in agreement.

"Are we done here?" Oskar asked. "I'm late for an important meeting."

Valentin stiffened at the thinly veiled insult, but I just smiled.

Oskar would have to do better than that if he wanted me to take offense. "I'm sure they won't mind starting without you," I said in my sweetest voice.

Myra burst into a spontaneous coughing fit that sounded a lot like suppressed laughter. Oskar flushed in anger but didn't do more than narrow his eyes at me. Coward.

I'd caught the attention of the other advisors, and I covertly gauged their reactions. None of them jumped to Oskar's defense. Hannah's expression turned disapproving, as if I were a child in need of discipline, but the others were more circumspect. I got the impression that Asmo also disapproved, but his true expression was harder to read behind the charming facade.

"You are dismissed," Valentin said sharply. "My afternoon meetings are canceled today. I will see you tonight at Queen Rani's welcome dinner."

Oskar grumbled something too low for me to catch, but Valentin stiffened and turned to him. "Did you have something to add, Advisor Krystopa?"

"No, Your Majesty," he said. "Until dinner." He bowed and left. The others followed suit, taking three of the four waiting transports.

"Well, they were lovely," I said once Valentin and I were alone with Luka and Imogen.

Valentin laughed. "Those were only my top advisors. There are dozens more just like them who fulfill lesser roles, but they don't report to me directly."

"Anyone I should especially keep an eye on?" I didn't want to tell Valentin that I'd done my own research until I got his opinion first.

"I'd put credits on Myra's loyalty, but I've been burned before," he said. "Everyone else is in play. None of them have made any obvious moves, and they all guard their communications closely."

Valentin had neural link abilities I'd never seen before. When I raised an eyebrow in question, his eyes flickered to Imogen before he said, "They are being extremely careful."

"Not exactly innocent behavior," I commented.

"No, but I need to figure out who is actively working against me and who is just looking out for number one."

"You could just fire them all and see who tries to kill you for it."

"If I did that, they would all try," Valentin said drily. He gestured toward the remaining transport. "Shall we?"

I'd been prepared to walk, but I supposed royalty didn't walk. Valentin and Luka loaded my trunks for me despite my assurance that I was perfectly capable of lifting a container full of clothes. I returned the sled to *Invictia* while Imogen waited with the transport and scanned our surroundings for threats.

Valentin had Luka, but if someone wanted him dead, he was far too exposed out in the open like this. A glance revealed at least a dozen vantage points where a sharpshooter would be close enough for a kill shot, but far enough away to escape detection.

"Do you monitor the surrounding buildings?" I asked when I returned to the waiting transport.

Valentin frowned for a second before his expression cleared. "Koan is safe."

I laughed at the absurdity. "Nowhere is safe if you have a price on your head. Do you mean to say that you've never had anyone try while you were here?"

"I appreciate your concern," he said, dodging the question. "Buildings and airspace facing the imperial grounds are both monitored, and we've stepped up security for the duration of your visit."

I let it go. He'd survived this long without my help, so perhaps he knew something I didn't. I made a mental note to discuss it with him later, when we were alone. Maybe he would be more forthcoming then.

————

THE TRANSPORT HUGGED the ground on the way to the palace, giving us an incredible view of the colorful gardens. Valentin pointed out the landmarks while Imogen and Luka scanned out the windows and surreptitiously watched each other.

The trees and shrubs opened, revealing a long stretch of green lawn. Valentin gestured to the circular stone folly in the distance. Marble columns held up a second-level balcony, and a domed third story offered a view of the garden. "My great-grandfather had that commissioned for my great-grandmother, to remind her of the architecture of her home. He—"

I caught a glint of white from under the dome of the folly. Before I could focus on it fully, Imogen shoved me to the floor and landed on top of me. Half a heartbeat later, Valentin landed next to me, Luka over him, and the transport jerked sideways. Bright yellow light flashed outside and a *boom* shook the vehicle.

Someone was shooting explosive rockets at us. "Tell me again how safe Koan is," I muttered to myself. The distinctive *thunk-sizzle* of plasma pulses raked the side of the transport facing the folly, but the reinforced windows and side panels held. For now.

Our attackers were shooting automatic, high-powered, long-range plasma rifles at us. Those types of weapons were expensive and hard to find outside the military. Not impossible, as evidenced by my armory in Arx, but not something amateurs would use. This was a precision strike, not an attack of opportunity.

The transport lurched sideways, then rapidly gained altitude as more explosions hit nearby. Flattened to the floor, I couldn't draw my pistol. I pressed up against Imogen, but she held her ground. "Stay down, Samara," she insisted. I stayed down. I wasn't sure that the floor was any safer, but at least I wouldn't be tossed about as the transport evaded the attack.

Luka and Valentin were strangely silent. I wiggled around until I could see both of them. Luka crouched over Valentin's prone form, plasma pistol drawn. His expression was intense and distant, but every time it flickered, the transport changed direction. He must've taken manual control via neural link, which meant I had him to thank for my continued existence.

Valentin's eyes were closed, but they moved rapidly behind his eyelids. A frown furrowed his forehead and his jaw clenched. Whatever he was doing was either difficult or painful. A few seconds later, I had my answer—it was *both*. A thin trickle of blood ran from his nose.

"Valentin, you're bleeding," I whispered.

"Almost there," he murmured. He winced and the bleeding increased. Just as I was becoming concerned, he opened his eyes. "Got them," he said with a savage grin. He looked up at Luka. "Team of six, in and around the folly, half the team is falling back to the northern edge of the park."

Luka nodded, but his expression didn't change. "I have two squads en route. I will let them know."

I rolled over and sat up, despite Imogen's unhappy protest. I'd never felt so useless or helpless. I burned with the need to *do* something, but trapped in the armored transport, there was nothing I *could* do. "How long until we're down?" I asked.

"Two minutes," Luka said without looking at me.

Two minutes might as well be two decades. The attackers would be long gone by the time I circled back, even if I left immediately, so hurrying wouldn't help. Hopefully Valentin's soldiers would catch one of them before they fled.

Valentin sat up and wiped away the blood. He caught my eye, then a second later, he sent me a neural link request. When I accepted, he said, *I'm sorry. I promised you safety and failed.*

I'm still alive, aren't I?

You know what I mean. I expected them to try something, but not so soon, and not so close to the palace. They should not have been able to infiltrate the folly without being noticed, either by patrols or drone sweeps. This is further proof that they have inside help.

That's why I'm here. Do you trust Luka?

With my life, he said. *He's had my back for longer than I've been emperor.*

I need to drop off my stuff, and then I want to check out the folly, to see if the attackers were careless enough to leave any clues. Unless you have video surveillance. Or trust your people to handle it and agree to answer my questions.

Valentin paused before saying, *The surveillance malfunctioned or was sabotaged. I will show you to your suite and then accompany you to the folly.*

So he didn't have video and he didn't trust his soldiers, at least not all of them. It wasn't entirely surprising, but it would make the afternoon more dangerous. It would be best if I could slip out on my own to do a little undercover recon.

The transport landed in an enclosed hangar. The door opened to reveal a squad of nine soldiers in Imperial Guard uniforms with weapons drawn. Luka and Valentin exited without hesitation, so I assumed these must be trusted guards and not a group here to murder us.

A man in his mid-thirties with light brown hair and brown eyes rushed up to us. "Valentin! I'm so glad you're okay. I coordinated teams to search the garden, as requested, and I'm working on the surveillance video."

"Thank you." Valentin turned to me. "Queen Rani, may I introduce my assistant, Lewis Birlow. Lewis, this is Queen Rani."

Lewis bowed low. "It is a pleasure to finally meet you." Unlike most of Valentin's advisors, Lewis seemed sincere. He was handsome, in a wholesome sort of way, with a willowy build and neatly pressed clothes.

I inclined my head. "It's nice to meet you, too."

My research hadn't been able to turn up much on Lewis. He'd worked with Valentin for years but generally kept to himself. There were a few old rumors of excessive spending, but I hadn't found anything recent to substantiate them.

Valentin and Lewis began discussing search patterns. Under her breath, Imogen asked, "Are you okay?"

"Yes. Thanks for protecting me. You spotted the threat before I did."

She smiled. "Changing locations is always risky, so I was on alert."

"I appreciate it. Valentin is going to show us to our room, then I'm heading out to the attack location to see what I can find. You're welcome to come with or stay here, your choice."

I expected her to grumble about the danger, but she just said, "Consider me your personal shadow for the duration of our trip."

3

After his discussion with Lewis wrapped up, Valentin led us to an enormous suite in the main building of the palace. "This is technically the family wing," he said, "but it's safer than the guest accommodations. And I'm just down the hall in case you need anything."

He said it without inflection, but the shadow of a grin he gave me had a wicked edge. It was the first sign he'd given that he, too, remembered our scorching kiss.

The living area ended in a wall of glass framing a balcony overlooking the garden. We were six stories up, which would deter casual outside entry but would do nothing to stop someone determined. As I approached, it became apparent that the windows were not actually glass, but were instead a thick, clear thermoplastic. They had to be high quality to look so much like normal glass.

"They're eight centimeters thick," Valentin said. "Rated to stop anything short of a missile. The palace is well defended. It's just everywhere else that is a concern." He muttered the last part under his breath.

I ventured deeper into the suite. It just kept going. A dining room, study, small kitchenette, and guest bath larger than my bedroom were to the right of the living room. To the left were three bedrooms, each with their own bathroom. Two of the bedrooms were identical, with balconies overlooking the park. The third was an interior room, but it had a wall display simulating the same outside view.

Valentin and Luka trailed behind me while Imogen swept the suite in front of us, looking for hidden threats. I doubted someone was waiting to jump out of a closet at me, but I let Imogen do her thing.

After we'd seen everything, I returned to the first bedroom with a balcony. The furniture was sleek and minimalist, made from what appeared to be dark, real wood. The walls were a hazy blue, nearly white, and the contrast made the room feel light and airy.

"Luka, why don't you show Ms. Weber the security features of the suite?" Valentin asked.

A wealth of nonverbal communication passed between them before Luka finally cocked his head at Imogen and grunted at her to follow.

She raised an eyebrow. "I don't understand caveman. You'll have to use your words."

If Luka was annoyed, I couldn't tell. He did expressionless better than anyone I'd ever met. "Ms. Weber, I kindly request the pleasure of your company," he said in a perfect, clipped upper-class accent, "while I show you how to prevent your principal from being murdered while you sleep."

His voice was as deep as I remembered, but that was not his native accent. Or it was, and what I'd heard before hadn't been. Either way, it was interesting.

If he'd been trying to insult Imogen, he'd failed spectacularly.

She ignored the implied insult and laughed. "Touché, Mr. Fox. And call me Imogen."

Luka just swept an arm toward the door, his expression lightly mocking. After looking to me and receiving a nod, she proceeded him from the room, an impish smile hovering about her lips. I silently wished her luck..

After they left, I moved closer to the window and glanced longingly at the balcony door. The floor-to-ceiling window offered a beautiful view of the gardens below, but the view would be even better from outside. Unfortunately, standing outside this soon after an attack would be unwise.

I was all too aware that, counterintuitively, the best time to strike sometimes came directly after a failed attempt. The target would be lulled into a false sense of safety because of all of the heightened security and make a stupid choice. If you could get past that security—which was often far easier than it should be— you had a clear shot at the target.

Taking Valentin out of the safety of the palace to inspect the folly would be one of those stupid choices, but I highly doubted I'd be able to talk him into staying while I went alone. We'd have to be extra careful.

Valentin came up beside me and stared at the garden. "Do you like the room?" he asked quietly.

I glanced at him, struck again by how handsome he was, starkly profiled against the bright wall. "It's lovely. Far more than I needed, but beautiful."

He turned to me and caught my hand, then slowly drew me close. When I came willingly, he enclosed me in a loose embrace. I laid my head on his shoulder—the shoulder that wasn't covered in medals. I touched a finger to the cool gold of an onyx-inlaid cross. I had no idea what it meant, but it seemed sad somehow, like it represented loss and heartbreak, rather than bravery and honor.

"I missed you," Valentin whispered into my hair.

"We talked nearly every day," I protested with a laugh. Then, softly, I admitted, "But I missed you, too."

"During the attack, all I could think about was how close you came to being hurt. I don't want you to get hurt helping me—once was enough. I think you should stick to an actual diplomatic visit."

I straightened and stepped back so I could see his face. "First of all, I was hurt in Arx because Commander Adams decided to attack. He would've attacked whether or not you were there, so you don't get to take responsibility for my injury. If not for your troops, it could've gone much worse."

The fact that we had needed rescue still galled a little. Ari had increased our defenses since the attack, but even so, we wouldn't be a match for a fleet of Quint warships.

"But—" Valentin started to protest.

I cut him off. "Second, I promised you help, and I intend to keep that promise. I knew it would be dangerous. I personally conned one or more of your advisors out of five million credits. They aren't going to let that go, even if my visit remains diplomatic."

In fact, I was somewhat surprised that they hadn't taken out a kill contract on me yet. Maybe they were hoping I was here to finish the job. Or maybe they knew I'd be an easier target here than in Arx.

Valentin sighed and ran a hand through his hair. "I didn't think it would work, but you can't blame me for trying," he said with a rueful grin. "I know you can take care of yourself. Hell, you busted me out of captivity. But I wouldn't be able to forgive myself if you were hurt again while trying to help me." He met my eyes, his voice low. "You're important to me."

Warmth and longing swirled through my system. I'd always been better at action than words, so I stood on tiptoe and brushed my lips across his, a fleeting caress that sent electric tingles skating along my nerves. His eyes darkened.

"You're important to me, too," I assured him quietly. "That's why I'm here. Who wants you dead, Valentin? Your half-brother Nikolas thinks you stole his crown. Is he working with your advisors or on his own? The Quint Confederacy would certainly like to see you dead. Who else?"

"That about sums it up: my brother, an unknown number of my advisors, and part of Quint. I don't know if they are working independently, together, or both. The note my advisors sent you came from the main administration building, but from one of the public terminals in the cafe. The surveillance logs were purged. Whoever they are, they are not stupid."

"I agree. I pulled all of the records I could on my own, but I couldn't get to any financial data. From what I've seen, there are lots of potentially shady deals happening, but that seems to be business as usual. Your advisors are all being very careful."

"*Can* you get financial data?"

"I can get anything for the right price, but a narrow search is better—and cheaper—than a wide one. I hoped to winnow the field before I called in the experts, especially because there is the minor risk of a double-cross. I trust the people I've worked with, but sometimes that trust gets broken." As evidenced by my former security specialist Jax.

Valentin looked thoughtful, but nodded his agreement.

While he was in such an agreeable mood, I broached my next concern. "I think you should stay here while I go check the folly. I can slip out unseen and be back before anyone realizes I'm gone."

"No." The denial was as hard as granite, with about as much give.

Imogen peeked into the room before I could figure out a persuasive enough argument to change his mind. "Is this the room you decided on?" she asked. When I nodded, she carried my first trunk of clothes inside. She glanced around, as if checking that no enemies had spawned from the ceiling before retreating for the second one.

"I think that means our time is up," Valentin said, deliberately changing the subject.

I let the argument go, for now. "I think you're right. And I know you don't like discussing the traitors, but I need all the information I can get if I'm going to help you."

"After dinner," he promised.

"Okay. Let me get changed, and then we'll go check the folly." He turned to leave, but I stopped him. "Wait, what's this medal for?" I asked, touching the black and gold cross.

His mouth flattened into a hard line. "Surviving," he said shortly. "I will wait for you in the living room." He bowed and left without another word.

———

I TRADED my flowing blouse for a stretchy, closer-fitting top and my heeled boots for military boots. With the slacks, I still looked presentable, but then I ruined the look by putting the holster on over my shirt.

The gun might raise some eyebrows, but the advantage of being royalty meant that most people wouldn't question a sovereign's weird eccentricities. Of course, that only worked if the person realized I *was* royalty—of a sort—which was questionable.

I slipped a knife into the sheath in my boot, then joined the others. In the living room, Imogen chattered at Luka. She wasn't normally a chatterbox, so she must be trying to annoy him. And judging from the tension in his jaw, it was working.

Valentin stood near the window, looking out, his gaze distant.

He turned to me when I approached. "I apologize for being short with you," he said softly.

I waved him off. "I'm sorry I dredged up bad memories."

"The Onyx Cross is awarded for extraordinary gallantry and heroism in battle," he said, his voice bitter. "Years ago, Father sent me to drive back the Quint Confederacy forces on Sag4. We didn't need the planet, had no settlers there, but he didn't want Quint to get a foothold. I went despite my reservations."

When he paused and didn't continue, I ventured, "It didn't go well?"

A laugh grated out of him. "It did *not* go well. I went in with a battalion. Five hundred soldiers. We should've outnumbered them five to one. Instead, we walked into a trap. They blew our ships out of the sky and my people were slaughtered. We took their command center and called for help, but by the time help arrived, I barely had a platoon left. Those men and women fought harder than anything I've ever seen, but Father only awarded the medal to me. I wear it for them."

He went from five hundred soldiers to less than thirty thanks to bad information. That was a heavy burden to bear, especially when he was then awarded a medal of heroism to really rub salt into the wound.

"I'm sorry," I said again. The words were hardly adequate, but they were all I had.

"Thank you," he said. He cleared his throat. "Are you ready to go see the attack site?"

"Did you capture any of the attackers?"

"Two," Valentin said. "They're in medical, and I've got trusted soldiers watching them while the docs try to patch them up."

"Any idea who they are?" I asked. A whole mercenary squad might work on a single kill contract if the bounty was high enough, but even then, they were usually far subtler than an open attack.

"The two we caught are not in any condition to talk. Neither has any identifying marks or documents, and facial recognition didn't turn up anything. We're searching for when they arrived. I've also got people trying to recover any surveillance video from the area."

"Who has the ability to disable the cameras?"

"The palace grounds are monitored and patrolled in shifts by three platoons of elite Kos soldiers. The Imperial Guard is responsible for everything inside the palace and my personal safety. Someone high enough in either organization could have disabled the cameras."

The military advisor, Oskar Krystopa, had already expressed his displeasure at my presence. He had been around since Valentin's father was emperor. He would've watched Nikolas grow up and had presumably made plans for when Nikolas became emperor. He had plenty of reason to want Valentin's brother on the throne rather than Valentin. I made a mental note to look at him more closely.

Myra Shah was the Imperial Guard advisor. She appeared the cleanest of the advisors, but perhaps that was just a careful front. Sometimes betrayal came from the most unexpected direction. "We need to question whoever was in charge today. After we visit the folly."

Valentin's mouth flattened into a hard line, but he nodded.

"Could Quint be behind it?" I asked. The attack felt like a military strike and not a kill contract strike—unless the merc squad was freshly out of the military and hadn't updated their strategy.

"They could be," Valentin said. "I'm not ruling anything out, but I'm not going to start flinging accusations without proof, either. I've spent months opening communications with Quint

Chairwoman Daniella Soteras, and an unfounded allegation could undo all of the progress I've made. Hopefully we'll know more after we question one of the men we caught."

I filed away the tidbit about talks with the Quint Confederacy's chairwoman. Soteras was in her early thirties and had been in control for a few years. She was rumored to be ruthless, but I held out hope that opening communication meant a peace treaty was possible in the future. "What about the rest of the attackers?"

"Escaped," Valentin said with a grimace.

"In that case, I really think you should stay in the palace today," I said. "The attackers have proven they can breach your defenses and get away. Going out is an unnecessary risk for you. It will be easier for me to slip out alone."

"And what if they were targeting you?"

"Then they shouldn't have missed the first time."

Valentin rolled his eyes, but a reluctant grin tipped up the corner of his mouth. While I'd been serious, sort of, I'd also been trying to wipe the sadness from his expression. Mission accomplished.

"How about a plan that ends with neither of us being shot?" he asked.

"Where's your sense of adventure?" When he just stared at me with a raised eyebrow, I relented. "Fine. What's your plan, then?"

"How important is it for you to see the attack site?"

"It's important. It's worth the risk for me, but less so for you." Valentin's mouth flattened into a stubborn line, so I didn't press the point. I continued, "I want a look at the sight lines at the very least. Can you see the spaceport from the folly, or did someone tip them off that we were on the move?"

"You can't see the spaceport," he said.

"Did your advisors take the same route?"

"No, they should've returned directly. I took you the long way to show off the gardens."

"Is that your usual route for visiting dignitaries?"

"Not usually, no." He anticipated where I was going. "Someone knew about my route in time to set up an ambush. It wasn't announced, but it wasn't exactly a secret, either. Probably a dozen or more people had access."

I resisted the urge to rub my forehead, barely. "You have a price on your head, Valentin. You need to be more careful."

His expression hardened and I caught a glimpse of the cunning warrior who lurked under the effortless charm, sarcastic wit, and polite manners. "I am not as easy to kill as they are hoping," he said.

He was right. He'd been under constant threat for at least a year and yet he still lived. Perhaps one day he'd trust me enough to confide how he'd managed it. I waited a beat, but he didn't elaborate. "Well, let's go test the gods of luck, then, shall we?"

4

Despite Valentin's apparent lack of concern for his personal safety, a squad of nine soldiers decked out in full Kos combat armor—visors open—awaited us in the hangar. They snapped to attention as we approached. Valentin saluted the dark-haired woman in front. "At ease, Sergeant Major."

She dropped into a rest pose with a smile. "Heard about this afternoon. Glad to see you're still kicking, sir," she said.

"You might be the only one, Sakimoto," Valentin said. He waved me forward. "This is Queen Samara Rani and her guard, Imogen Weber. I want you to keep an eye on them today. Samara, this is Sergeant Major Natalie Sakimoto. She'll keep you safe."

At first glance, I put her age in the late twenties because her face was unlined and her hair was solid black. But when I met her eyes, I revised my guess up by a decade. She had the quiet confidence that came with time and experience. She was pretty, with a wide face that narrowed to a delicate chin. She had a compact, muscular frame and lightly tanned skin.

She bowed. "Queen Rani, Ms. Weber, it's nice to meet you both."

I held out my hand for a handshake. After a brief hesitation, she took it. Her handshake was firm without being overbearing. I liked her already.

"Nice to meet you, Sergeant Major," I said. "I don't stand on ceremony. Call me Samara."

She grinned at me. "Samara, feel free to call me Natalie or Sakimoto, whichever you prefer. Have you worn combat armor before?"

I knew combat armor was safer, but I felt blind and deaf with it on. "Do you have a helmet and vest I can use instead? And if you have a scoped plasma rifle, I'll take one of those, too. Preferably a Remy MK9 if you have one."

Her eyebrows crept up her forehead. "You want a specialty sniper rifle?" she asked.

"If you have one," I agreed mildly. "If not, I'll take any decent long-range rifle with a scope."

Natalie looked to Valentin, and he nodded his permission without asking a single question as to *why* I needed a sniper rifle. The man was entirely too trusting.

"I'll have to pull one from the armory," Natalie said. "It'll take ten minutes. Let's get everyone suited up while we wait."

I accepted an incoming neural link from Imogen. *What are you up to?* she asked without looking at me.

Just covering the bases, I replied. *Might be nothing.*

———

IN THE END, Imogen talked me into wearing a full set of prototype armor, though I kept my visor open. The armor had the built-in active camouflage ability that had allowed the Quint soldiers attacking Arx to appear invisible. If we were attacked at the folly, being able to disappear into thin air would be a decided advantage.

We took two armored troop transports. They had vid screens instead of windows, complete with thermal imaging overlays. The software was smart enough to fade the colors of expected background temperatures and only highlight abnormalities.

Such as the person-shaped red blob we were currently passing. The video showed a patch of empty grass, but the thermal image was another story.

I pointed it out to Natalie. She said, "One of ours. You'll see more as we get closer."

"How do you know they're yours?"

She tapped her closed visor. "My soldiers' locations are tagged on my display. And I'm the one who sent him there. The transport software also knows he's friendly. Jordan, turn off your transponder for a ten count."

A few seconds later, a warning sounded and a red box appeared around the soldier on the display until he reengaged his transponder. Interesting technology and far superior to anything we had in Arx, but it seemed like it would be fairly easy to override.

"What prevents someone from stealing a transponder?" Imogen asked, sharing my concerns.

"They're secured when not in use," Natalie said. "As a safety precaution, today I manually flagged the approved transponders after verifying my soldiers were still in possession. Someone could kill a soldier and take their approved armor, but that would generate different warnings."

"Were these soldiers out during the attack?" I asked.

"I'm not at liberty—" she started.

"Two squads were deployed around the spaceport and adjacent buildings," Valentin cut in. "The rest of the park, including the folly, was covered by the standard security patrols."

I frowned at him. He hadn't told me about the soldiers when I'd asked. He caught my expression and linked to me. *Koan is generally very safe, but I'm not stupid. The two of us together are a tempting target. I would not gamble with your safety.*

Why didn't you tell me?

I didn't want you to worry.

Then you failed because I was worried that you were running around without any security, I said. *Figuring out what happened, who attacked and why, is my wheelhouse, but I can't help you if you don't give me all the information. With soldiers on patrol, either the attackers were in place early or the patrols themselves were compromised. That makes a difference. I need you to trust me, at least with this.*

I do trust you, but I am not used to sharing. I will try, he promised, then closed the link.

I understood where he was coming from. When secrecy meant survival, you learned to keep everything close. It was something I had struggled with for years, especially after I first became queen. I had tried to do everything and be everywhere because I didn't trust others enough to let them in.

The fact that I *couldn't* do everything had been a hard lesson to learn.

Our transport landed on the edge of the manicured lawn surrounding the stone folly. Before Natalie opened the door, she checked with her teams on the ground and in the surrounding buildings. The site was as secure as they could make it.

I would still be keeping a wary eye on my surroundings.

Up close, the folly was bigger than I expected, close to fourteen meters from the ground to the top of the dome and ten meters in diameter. The second level was held up by eight stone columns and two curved staircases that spiraled down in the middle of the circular structure. The second-story balcony had a beautifully carved stone balustrade that provided minimal cover.

So why had the attackers chosen this building?

I circled the perimeter, looking for a clue to their thinking, but nothing obvious came to light. I *might* have chosen this building for a one-person sniper strike, but for an entire team? There had to be better options.

I looked back toward the palace, where our transport had been attacked. I could just see the scorched earth where an explosive round had landed. I tilted my head, gauging distance. Perhaps they had picked this building because it was at the limit of the range on their ordnance. A plasma rifle could easily cover this distance and more, but I was less familiar with explosive weapons.

"What is it?" Valentin asked.

"Do you know what they were shooting at us? It seemed like an explosive rocket of some type. Does it have a range of four hundred meters?"

"Most shoulder-launched plasma rockets have a point range around four hundred meters," Natalie said.

"Do they cause damage like that?" I asked, pointing to the disrupted ground.

"Yes, if they miss."

"And if they'd hit our transport?"

Her tone was grim. "We wouldn't be having this conversation. Valentin's transports are armored, but those weapons are designed to pierce armor. You might've survived, but you would've been in medical for a long time."

I turned to Valentin. "Did you plan your exact route or have someone else do it?"

"I did." He paused. "But Lewis handled coordination with security." Desolation haunted his expression for an instant before cold fury chased it away. "He has been with me since before I became emperor."

I touched his arm, though I doubted he could feel it through the thick armor. "He might be innocent," I said quietly. "You said others had access. Don't jump to conclusions." But even as I spoke, I made a mental note to dig deeper into his assistant. I hadn't gotten any weird vibes from the man, but compromising someone so close to the emperor would provide a gold mine of information.

Valentin stepped closer and tipped his head down to mine. My breath caught at the intent look in his eyes. Luka cleared his throat. Valentin stopped and straightened, then murmured, "Thank you."

I wanted to haul him back and kiss him again, but we had an audience that was pretending not to look at us while also keeping us firmly in view. Luka wasn't being an asshole; he was looking out for Valentin. It would do Valentin no favors to be romantically linked to the Rogue Queen. Still, it stung.

"You're welcome," I said with a too-bright smile. "Ready to check the upper levels?"

Valentin frowned at me, but when I shook my head a fraction, he let it go. "Lead on," he said.

I approached the empty folly with Imogen, Valentin, Luka, and Natalie trailing behind me. A meter from the building, between one step and the next, a dozen soldiers appeared inside, seemingly from thin air. I had my gun drawn before I recognized their Kos armor and lack of visible weapons. I hesitated just as Natalie shouted, "Don't shoot!"

I took a deep breath and let the adrenaline work its way through my system. "That was not smart," I said. "I could've shot one of your people. You should've warned me."

"You're far faster than I gave you credit for," she agreed. "I didn't think you'd go straight for your weapon."

I couldn't see her expression through her visor, but she sounded calm. She had known the soldiers were there, hidden behind active camouflage. I fought to keep my own voice level. "Attacks tend to make me twitchy," I said, "so when a bunch of unknown soldiers appear, my instinct is to shoot first. By withholding information, you put your soldiers' lives in my hands." And stars knew my hands had enough blood on them already.

"According to command, you are a security concern," Natalie said. "The soldiers are armored. Command wanted to see how you would react to a threat and deemed it an acceptable risk. I disagreed but was overruled."

"My pistol rounds would've punched straight through their armor at this distance. If even one of them had been holding a weapon pointing at me, they would be dead." I turned to Valentin. "Did you know about this?"

"No," he said, his voice cold.

Ice slid down my spine. If Valentin didn't have control of the military, then he didn't have control of the Empire, and a military commander testing a foreign dignitary without prior approval from the emperor seemed like a distinct lack of control.

Just how tenuous was his position?

Worry hardened into resolve. Valentin would remain the Kos Emperor, even if I had to personally kill every one of his traitorous advisors to make it happen. They were right to think of me as a security concern, but they were stupid to reveal their hand so early.

They had no idea what I could do, what I *would do,* to protect what was mine—and for now, Valentin Kos was mine.

Next to me, Imogen still had her plasma pistol drawn, though she kept it pointed at the ground. It was one thing to underestimate me, but to underestimate me *and* my bodyguard was either incredibly stupid or an attempt to set up an intergalactic incident.

"You fucked up, Sergeant Major Sakimoto," I said. "Not command, *you*. You put your soldiers' lives at risk."

"I have to follow orders, ma'am." She kept her tone polite, but frustration seeped through.

"You could have discussed it with me," Valentin said. "Why didn't you?"

"I was ordered not to warn either of you."

"By whom?"

"By Commander Young. But I believe the original order came from Advisor Krystopa."

5

"Oskar Krystopa ordered you to test my diplomatic guest without my knowledge?" Valentin clarified, his tone dangerous.

"As far as I know, sir," Natalie said. She stood at attention and wouldn't meet Valentin's eyes. "Commander Young grumbled about it."

"And despite the fact that I personally asked you to keep Queen Rani safe, you continued to follow his orders over mine?"

Natalie flushed red. "Queen Rani was never in any danger. All soldiers were warned not to return fire in the event things went sideways."

"The fact that you even had to give them that order meant you knew things *could* go sideways," Valentin growled. "Why did you go ahead with it?"

Natalie seemed frozen in place, but Valentin waited her out. Finally, she met his eyes, then frowned.

"Answer aloud," Valentin said. "Queen Rani deserves to hear your reasoning."

She cast a faintly apologetic glance my way before staring

straight ahead. Her tone was subdued. "From what I heard, Advisor Krystopa believes Queen Rani is a threat. Commander Young disagreed, but he approved the test because it came with permission to use the active camouflage veil units, which increased site security for you. He was worried about snipers, sir."

Sakimoto did not sound like someone who wanted Valentin gone. Oskar remained a wildcard, but perhaps the military as a whole wasn't as lost as I thought.

"I will speak to Commander Young and Advisor Krystopa," Valentin promised. Based on his tone, I would not want to be at the other end of that conversation. "Queen Rani is not a threat, and even if she were, that is not for you to decide. From now on, you will disclose any orders that may affect me or my guests. That is a direct order. Do not fail me again, Sergeant Major."

She snapped a precise salute. "Yes, sir. I'm sorry, sir." She glanced at me out of the corner of her eye. "I'm sorry, ma'am."

"You should be," Imogen snapped. She was not wrong, and Luka nodded along with her.

Valentin turned to me. His visor was open but his face was unreadable. "I apologize," he said formally. "Thank you for your restraint."

"It was a near thing. I hope you make it very clear to Advisor Krystopa that he nearly got a soldier killed today. He may not like me, but his orders were reckless."

"It will be crystal clear," Valentin vowed darkly.

"And then thank him for showing off your stellar active camouflage tech. I didn't know it could cover entire buildings."

A reluctant grin bloomed on Valentin's face. "Only small buildings."

I looked over my shoulder. I could see the transport behind us. I stepped back and crossed through the invisible line of the veil. The soldiers in the folly disappeared, hidden behind the projection of an empty folly. When I stepped forward again, they reappeared. I'd seen Kos active camouflage in use in Arx when the Quint Confederacy had attacked, so I'd known it was good, but I hadn't known it was *this* good.

"Does the veil protect the upper levels as well?" I asked.

"Yes," Natalie said. She had retreated behind a wall of ice. I didn't blame her much. Being dressed down by the emperor in front of your troops had to sting, even if she knew it could've been much worse. People had been convicted of treason for less.

At least we wouldn't have to worry about distant shooters thanks to the camouflage. I could almost see Commander Young's side of things, especially if he truly didn't think I was a threat to his troops.

"Did the shots come from the second or third level?"

"Both," Luka and Imogen said at the same time. He waved for Imogen to continue. She said, "The rockets came from the third level, but the plasma rifles were shot from the second floor." Luka nodded in agreement.

"Okay, then let's see what we can see."

In the middle of the folly, two sets of curving stairs spiraled up like a double helix around a solid central column. The staircases were beautifully carved out of what appeared to be solid marble. The vast amount of wealth displayed in this little building— nothing more than a pretty landscape piece—boggled the mind. I could feed my people for six months for less than the cost of the staircase alone.

On the second floor, an arched doorway opened out to the south side of the balcony. From here, I had a better vantage point to the attack site. I released the sniper rifle from my back. At nearly fifteen kilograms, the MK9 wasn't exactly light. It was designed to be shot from a prone position, with a bipod on the front to hold the gun steady on the ground. In a pinch, the bipod could be propped on a railing, and I could also shoot freestanding with decent accuracy thanks to my strength augments, but when maximum accuracy was needed, nothing beat lying prone.

Because I didn't plan on shooting anything, I remained standing and sighted the target area through the scope. There was a fairly small gap between the trees and shrubs where the transport would've been visible.

Waiting in a state of high alert was mentally and physically taxing, but they'd gotten a shot off less than ten seconds after our transport had appeared. We were either dealing with an elite team or they'd had another lookout, someone who had tipped them off that we were on the move.

I swung the gun toward the spaceport. Valentin was right; it wasn't visible through the trees. Perhaps they didn't have a sharpshooter on the team, so they'd picked this building because it provided some cover and was close enough to our route for explosive rounds. The gardens also provided plenty of opportunity to disappear once the attack was over.

But it just didn't feel right. Was I missing something or was I thinking too much like a lone assassin and not enough like a military unit?

"What do you see?" Valentin asked.

"Questions," I muttered. "Let's check upstairs."

The third floor didn't shed any new light on the attack. From here, I could just see the tops of the largest spaceships in the palace spaceport, but that wouldn't be enough to target someone on the ground. Most of the buildings to our north were dozens of stories tall. I carefully checked the rooflines with my scope, but they were clear.

Valentin had tagged the attackers as a team of six. Two were caught and four escaped. Perhaps the remaining four hadn't had time to regroup and try for a second attack, but this was a perfect opportunity—one an experienced mercenary crew wouldn't have wasted. The more I learned, the more I realized these weren't normal mercenaries or assassins.

So who were they?

———

AFTER INSPECTING THE FOLLY, Valentin, Luka, Imogen, and I headed to the command center for the palace grounds. A man in his late forties in the red-and-black dress uniform of the Kos Empire and with a chest full of medals met us at the door.

"Emperor Kos." He greeted Valentin with a wary bow and then nodded at me. "Queen Rani."

"Commander Young." Valentin's voice was arctic.

Ah, here was the man responsible for my so-called test. It would be handy if traitors had some sort of visible aura, but Commander Young looked like every other military commander I'd met: fit, serious, and hard-edged.

"Join me in my office?" Young asked.

Valentin inclined his head a fraction of a centimeter. He was as cold and distant as a frozen moon.

Young led us through the command center. More than a dozen people in military uniforms were scattered at workstations in the middle of the room. Offices and conference rooms lined the walls, clearly visible behind clear glass windows and doors. Young led us to a corner office. The wall facing the room was frosted glass rather than clear. Privacy must be one of the perks of command.

Luka and Imogen entered with us and stood by the door. On the way over, we'd talked about leaving them outside, but if Young was compromised, then armed backup was a good idea.

Valentin took a seat in one of the two chairs in front of the desk. I remained standing. Commander Young hesitated, then settled behind his desk, his gaze on Valentin.

"You will answer Queen Rani's questions," Valentin said. "And then you and I will discuss your treason."

"I never—"

"Silence." The word cracked like thunder and Young snapped his mouth shut. Valentin turned to me. "Whenever you are ready, Queen Rani."

My smile was not kind and Young tensed. "Are you augmented, Commander?"

Young looked at Valentin but only received a hard stare in return. He sighed and answered, "I am."

"So you know how fast augmented soldiers are, and yet you still decided to test me directly after I'd been attacked, when I was trigger-happy and high on adrenaline. Do you care so little for your soldiers' lives?"

"I did as I was ordered," he grated out.

"Who gave the order?"

"Advisor Oskar Krystopa."

Young knew how to play the game. He was answering my questions, but with as little information as he could get away with. It was time to see if I could shake him up.

"Were you aware that I was a mercenary before I became queen?"

His lip curled in a derisive sneer. "Yes."

"And were you aware that I rescued Emperor Kos from the Quint forces holding him hostage?"

The sneer was replaced with a look of faint surprise. "No, I was not."

"Who told you I was a mercenary?"

"Advisor Krystopa."

Of course. I'm sure the part where I'd saved Valentin's life multiple times had merely slipped Krystopa's mind. If I'd wanted Valentin Kos dead, he would be dead. I wouldn't have needed to plan an elaborate plot in the capital city. I'd had him in my grasp and let him go, unharmed.

Krystopa's claim that I was dangerous to Valentin was built entirely on fiction.

"Why was the surveillance system down?"

Young glanced at Valentin once again and got a nod in return. The commander grimaced. "The system is undergoing maintenance for upgrades. It was supposed to be done last week, but the crew is behind schedule."

"How extensive is the outage?"

"Zone 15 extends from the palace to the edge of the park, including the folly."

"You knew Valentin was going to pass through a dark zone. Why wasn't he warned?"

"Teams swept the entire zone while you were entering the atmosphere."

I leaned over his desk. "Have you questioned the team responsible for sweeping the folly?"

"The four soldiers were questioned independently. They all swear the folly was empty."

So the attackers had either moved in after the sweep, or all four of Valentin's soldiers were compromised. If the attackers had known about the sweep, then that still meant that someone had alerted them. Rooting out traitors was difficult because there were so many possibilities.

I stayed where I was, so Young would have to look up at me looming over him. "Who ordered the surveillance upgrades?"

He held my gaze. "Advisor Krystopa."

"How many people knew about the outages?"

"Everyone in the chain of command from Advisor Krystopa

down and most of the teams. We always schedule extra patrols when the electronics are down. We alerted Valentin's assistant, too, but he approved because the emperor wanted to show you the gardens."

I barely managed to hold in the sigh that wanted to escape. Maybe no one in the Kos Empire actually wanted Valentin dead, and instead, they were all just horribly incompetent. Still, there were too many coincidences here, and all roads led back to Oskar Krystopa.

I leaned back. "Do you believe that Advisor Krystopa is loyal to Emperor Kos?"

"Yes." Young's expression didn't even flicker—he either believed what he was saying or he was the best liar ever.

"Have you worked with Advisor Shah at all?"

"Rarely. I usually work with Commander Grant if I am working with the Imperial Guard. The Guard isn't part of the military directly, but Grant is my equivalent in their organization."

"Do you believe that Commander Grant is loyal to Emperor Kos?"

Young paused in thought. "She's never given me any reason to believe otherwise, but I've only worked with her occasionally."

"Did she know about the surveillance maintenance?"

"Yes."

I turned to Valentin. "He's all yours. Thank you."

"You're welcome. I will meet you later, after I've dealt with *this*." Valentin waved a negligent hand at Young, but his menacing expression belied his nonchalance. Silently, he linked me to add, *Be careful. Stay safe.*

6

After Valentin spoke to Commander Young and Advisor Krystopa, he was pulled into an urgent meeting. Left to my own devices, I used the afternoon to wander the grounds and smuggle in my trunk full of weapons and gear. Imogen shadowed me, but we didn't run into any trouble.

Unfortunately.

Now it was time to face the wolves at dinner. My evening gown was gorgeous, with an off-the-shoulder bodice that flared into a wide skirt. It flattered my petite figure while also giving me a pocket for my plasma pistol. The stunning sapphire blue fabric draped like silk and protected like light armor. I'd loved this dress when I first tried it on, but I still thought the price was ridiculous. Ari and Stella had both told me it was worth it.

I left my long hair down. It was naturally wavy, so the dark brown strands curled over my bare shoulders without the need for a curling iron. I lined my eyes with a heavy black liner and applied smoky eyeshadow. This dress wasn't meant for meek makeup.

After I finished getting ready, I practiced drawing and

holstering my pistol a few times until I could do it without looking. I'd already been shot at once today. Next time, I wanted to be
able to shoot back.

A knock on the suite door announced Valentin's arrival. "I'll
get it!" Imogen called.

I firmly quashed the flutter of nervous anticipation. I wasn't
going to get nervous just because I had a pretty dress and makeup
on. I turned in front of the mirror to check that my pistol was
concealed.

It really was a beautiful dress.

In the living room, Imogen spoke to Luka in a low tone. She
had traded out her blouse and slacks for a simple black dress that
hugged her figure. Luka wore a black suit and looked a little shell-
shocked.

I caught sight of Valentin and my heart skipped a beat. He had
on a three-piece charcoal suit with a white shirt and a striped
silver tie. His dark hair fell over his forehead and he hadn't
shaved the stubble from his jaw. He had always been objectively
gorgeous—the Kos dynasty had access to the best genetics money
could buy—but tonight he had a rough edge that made him even
sexier.

He glanced up, caught sight of me, and froze. Several emotions
crossed his face, too fast to track, before he crossed the room to
me. He took my hand and bowed over it. "Good evening, my lady,"
he murmured. He straightened but kept my hand. Desire smol-
dered in his eyes. "Samara, you are stunning."

My pulse kicked. If he kept staring at me like I was the most
beautiful woman in the universe, we might not make it to dinner.
"Thank you. You look incredible, too. Even without your imperial
regalia," I teased, trying to find my way back to solid ground.

He smiled and brushed a feather-light kiss across my knuckles,
then reluctantly let go of my fingers. "The one nice thing about

being emperor is the ability to set dinner dress," he said. "No regalia required."

"Must be nice. Stella bullied me into buying this dress despite the fact that it cost more than the new hull shielding for *Invictia*."

"Remind me to send Stella a token of my appreciation," he said.

I laughed and shook my head. "Don't. She's already impossible to live with," I said affectionately. "If she finds out how much I like this dress, she'll be unbearably smug."

"She deserves to be unbearably smug," he said. He held out an elbow. "Shall we?"

I hooked my hand through his arm. "How many people are going to be at dinner?" I asked.

"I'm hosting official dinners while you are here, both to show my support and to give you a chance to interact with my advisors. My whole court is invited to official dinners, so close to a hundred people, but you really only need to worry about a dozen or so."

"The advisors I met this morning?"

"Yes, and their spouses, and a few other key people."

"Sounds delightful," I lied.

Valentin grinned before he turned serious. "We don't have to go. I can order dinner brought here."

Temptation, thy name was Valentin Kos. I squeezed his arm. "That means a lot to me, but we're going. I want to know who shot at us. I want you to be safe in your own home, even if that home is a ridiculous palace."

―――――

WE TOOK the elevator down to the second floor, then Valentin led us through a series of labyrinthine passageways until we popped out in front of a tall set of double doors flanked by a pair of young men in imperial servant uniforms. They bowed to Valentin.

"Ready?" Valentin asked. When I inclined my head, he gestured to the servants. They turned in perfect sync and opened the door.

The doorway revealed a wide set of marble steps leading down into a massive ballroom. A crowd circulated below, clustered in little gossiping groups. The women wore colorful evening gowns and piles of expensive, sparkling jewels. The men wore suits or tuxedos ranging from somber black to bright violet. They all turned as we were announced by the uniformed attendant at the top of the stairs. "His Imperial Majesty Emperor Valentin Kos of the Kos Empire and Her Majesty Queen Samara Rani of the Rogue Coalition."

Silence descended on the room, swift and absolute.

I had debated whether I should attempt to pass myself off as a naive simpleton, but any advisors worth their salt should've done research on me—just as I had done on them. Most of the information about my past was buried, but one didn't become queen of a bunch of rogues by being stupid. If I played dumb, they would know I was up to something.

Instead, I'd decided to go for coolly arrogant and aloof. It was closer to my natural personality than wide-eyed innocence, so it would be easier to maintain. And nothing bothered people as much as not being able to read their opponent. With that in mind, I affixed a neutral expression to my face and looked around in apparent boredom as Valentin escorted me down the steps.

Boredom was difficult to fake because the ballroom was incredible. The soaring ceiling was painted in a series of murals depicting ancient, stylized battles that told the story of the rise of the Kos Empire. Heavy, embroidered draperies lined the walls and three massive chandeliers provided soft illumination. Servants in imperial uniforms wove through the crowd with trays of champagne and tiny appetizers.

At the bottom of the steps, Myra Shah, the head of the Imperial Guard, waited for our arrival. She wore a deep amber sheath dress that complemented her dark hair and golden skin. She dipped into a shallow curtsy as we approached. "Your Majesties," she said.

I would never get used to someone calling me 'majesty.' The fact that I was grouped in the same category as Valentin was laughable, and evidently I wasn't the only one who thought so. Sound returned as a low rumble of voices, and most of them didn't sound welcoming.

"Myra," I greeted, "it's nice to see you again."

She launched into polite small talk at the same time I got a group neural link request from an unknown contact. Valentin was the third person in the group and when I caught Myra's eye, she nodded very slightly, while not pausing in her chatter.

Holding two conversations at once was a skill not too many people possessed. The human brain wasn't designed to focus so heavily on two things at once. It took a lot of practice, but I wouldn't be too surprised if all of Valentin's advisors could do it. I'd learned how to do it because it was a handy—and underhanded—skill to have.

I accepted the link as I murmured the correct responses to the small talk.

Rumor has it that the attack this afternoon was Rogue Coalition rebels attempting a coup, Myra said without preamble. *Is there any possibility it is true?*

No, I said flatly. I'd heard no rumors of unrest anywhere in the Rogue Coalition, and I would've if they'd existed. *Someone is setting me up.*

I thought so, she said. *Everything I've heard indicates that you're beloved by your people.*

I did my best to ensure my people's happiness, and in return, they gave me their loyalty. Perhaps that was close enough to being beloved, especially when compared to Valentin's court.

Aloud, Myra had switched from the weather to the ballroom. I commented on the murals and Valentin launched into their history. It seemed we all could focus on both conversations at once.

Who started the rumor? Valentin asked.

I don't know yet, Myra said. *I've got a few people looking into it, but the first I heard of it was when I arrived tonight, otherwise I would've given you more warning.*

Thank you, I said.

Let me know as soon as you find anything, Valentin said.

Myra agreed and closed the link. When Valentin finished his mural explanation, she bobbed another curtsy and took her leave.

I opened a link to Valentin. When he accepted, I asked, *How long until dinner? There will be dinner, right?*

Yes, dinner will be served in an hour.

In that case, I need you to go get me a drink. Take your time; I want to see who smells blood in the water. And if you can, listen in on your advisors.

Valentin's eyes flashed with suppressed temper, even as he smiled at my compliments on the ballroom. *If I leave you, it will look like I am withdrawing my support.*

Even better, I said. *You know I can handle myself. And what people say to me alone will be far more interesting than what they say when you're around. I may say some things you won't like to provoke a response. Let me know if any of them get back to you.*

I could practically *feel* his reluctance to leave me alone across our link, but he nodded very slightly. Subtly, his demeanor changed. He looked around as if he were looking for an escape, and his posture slowly went rigid and unwelcoming. Spotting someone in the crowd, he gave me a stiff bow. "Excuse me, my lady, but I see someone I must speak with. *Alone.*"

He walked off without another word, but across our link he said, *Be careful. I will be monitoring the situation, but link me or shout if you need help.*

If we hadn't discussed it, I would've truly thought he was trying desperately to escape me. Note to self: Valentin was a hell of an actor.

Thank you, I said then closed the link. I needed to focus on a single conversation. Valentin's advisors were unlikely to walk up and announce they were traitors. It certainly would speed things along if they did, though.

Asmo Copley, the advisor for domestic affairs, was the first to pounce. He sidled up to me and put a hand on my—thankfully covered—lower back. My skin crawled, and I held onto my indifferent mask by sheer force of will. I couldn't put my finger on it, but something about him set off all of my internal alarm bells, and I always trusted my gut.

"Advisor Copley, to what do I owe the pleasure?" I asked flatly.

He beamed at me. The man was blindingly handsome in his dark tuxedo, and he used that beauty as a weapon. "Call me Asmo, my darling," he said.

Ugh. He was the spoiled son of a wealthy family. I doubted very many people in his life had ever told him no. I'd happily be the first.

He continued in a conspiratorial whisper, "I believe you may have offended our fearless leader. I don't know what you said, but I've never seen him so eager to leave a beautiful woman's side before."

I glanced away in disinterest. Out of the corner of my eye, I saw Asmo's smile go tight. Oh, he didn't like to be ignored. I waved a negligent hand. "Valentin needed to speak to someone. He will return when he is finished."

Asmo leaned close, forcing my attention back to him. I clenched my fist against the urge to smash his perfect nose and reclaim my space. "I don't know how it works in the Rogue Coalition, but here, we don't leave our honored guests to fend for themselves in a crowd," he said, his words dripping with thinly veiled condescension. "I will escort you until he returns."

I'd rather eat glass, but I kept my expression bland. "As you wish."

7

Rather than offering me an elbow, Asmo guided me around the room with his hand on my lower back. Forcefully removing said hand would probably get me arrested, so I just *thought* about it. Perhaps the thoughts were a little too obvious because the group in front of us stopped talking mid-sentence.

Do you want me to remove him? Imogen linked. *If not, tone down the murderous expression. You're scaring the locals.*

I smiled and the people around me relaxed. *Leave him be. It's better if he thinks I'm weak and easily manipulated by his dazzling good looks. Rumor has it that the attack was Rogue Coalition rebels.*

I could hear her mental snort across the link. *Someone is spreading lies. And if his hand slides any lower, I'm breaking it,* she promised. *He should learn some respect.*

Agreed. I closed the link. I could break his hand myself, but that would ruin the whole persona I was trying to pull off. It would be better for Imogen to do it, but less fun for me.

Asmo introduced me to a few more people before leading me toward a cluster of the advisors I'd met this morning. Oskar

Krystopa led military strategy, Joanna Cook advised science and technology, and Hannah Perkins was in charge of diplomatic relations.

They were standing with three people whom I hadn't met, but I recognized two of them from my research. The older, white-haired gentleman was Hannah's husband. They had been married for decades. Beside them stood Oskar's stunning daughter. She shared his curly black hair and green eyes. Rumor had it he was grooming her to take over his advisor position. The only person I didn't recognize stood next to Joanna. He was an attractive, middle-aged man, and judging by their closeness, they were lovers.

As we approached, Oskar scowled, Joanna ignored me, and Hannah looked entirely too smug. Their companions took their clues from the group and gave me chilly glares of their own, with the exception of Oskar's daughter. She smiled at me.

It even seemed genuine.

They were all dressed in expertly tailored designer clothes. Hannah wore a long black and silver gown that perfectly matched her husband's silver tie. Oskar was dressed in all black: black suit, black shirt, black tie. The monochromatic clothing made his green eyes pop. His daughter had followed his lead and wore a black A-line gown. Joanna had on a gorgeous red mermaid gown and had piled her blond hair up in curls on top of her head. Her lover hadn't gotten the memo and wore a dark suit with a navy tie. The ladies dripped with enough jewels to feed everyone in Arx for weeks.

"Hello, dear," Hannah said. "I do hope the rumor we're hearing about you isn't true." Her tone indicated just the opposite. She had to be in her seventies or eighties, but she hadn't lost any of her bite. She also didn't bother to introduce me to her companions—a subtle snub.

"That depends on the rumor," I said. "There are plenty of rumors about me that are absolutely true."

"They say the attack this afternoon was Rogue Coalition rebels attempting a coup. Is it true that you're facing a rebellion at home?" she asked with a shark's smile.

"If I were, do you think I would be stupid enough to confirm it to the emperor's advisors?" I asked coolly.

"You will if Valentin's life is at risk," Oskar growled. "Or I'll have you deported."

"Father," his daughter chided softly.

I narrowed my eyes at him. I had many reasons to suspect Oskar Krystopa and none to believe him, but he sounded strangely sincere. I'd learned to trust my gut, but I decided to press him a little, to see what he would do.

"Try it," I said with an unruffled smile. "Valentin would never allow it, as you no doubt learned this afternoon. He's quite enamored with me." I let my sly expression and tone imply that I had Valentin wrapped securely around my finger. I wondered just how long it would take to get back to him. Based on Oskar's expression, I'd guess less than five minutes, but the other three advisors were harder to read. Oskar's daughter looked strangely disappointed.

"I believe you are vastly overestimating your power," Hannah said. "Valentin left you alone in a crowded foreign ballroom. If Asmo hadn't rescued you, you would've been left adrift."

Even Joanna was paying attention now. She watched me with a calculating expression. If she expected me to give up and apologize, she was about to be disappointed.

"I believe you are *underestimating* my power. Valentin left to speak to an acquaintance on a business matter that I had no interest in," I said with a dismissive flick of my fingers. "And I am never adrift; I am always exactly where I mean to be."

Hannah gave me a patronizing little pat. "If you say so, dear."

"I can make you disappear without a trace," Oskar threatened. "Valentin doesn't even have to know, so whatever power you think you have is worthless."

Well, now, wasn't *that* interesting. Oskar might not be an outright traitor, but he was definitely undermining Valentin's authority. And this time, his daughter didn't come to my defense.

Imogen stepped up beside me. "Do not threaten Queen Rani," she said.

"Or what? You'll fuss at me and tell me to mind my manners?" Oskar scoffed. He'd made the mistake of judging Imogen based on her appearance.

She had opened a neural link with me before he'd finished speaking. *May I?* she asked.

Yes, but don't hurt him.

She closed the link and had Oskar on the floor before he'd even realized she was moving. She hadn't touched any of the others standing in our little circle. "No, Advisor Krystopa, I will not fuss at you. I will kill you," she promised. "This is your only warning."

Excited murmurs spread from our location. It appeared that this was the most entertaining thing to happen at an official dinner in *ages*.

"You will pay for this!" Oskar hissed. "Let me up."

Imogen looked to me. "Let him up," I said. "I believe he's learned his lesson."

Oskar stood and angrily straightened his suit. If looks could kill, his would strike me dead. "I will have you deported tonight," he promised. He stormed off before I could bait him further. His daughter tossed me another disappointed look before she turned and followed her father.

"That was poorly done, my dear," Hannah murmured with a disapproving frown. "You should control your people."

"Imogen acted with my blessing."

Hannah tutted at me. "Then perhaps you should control yourself."

The fact that she was still well enough to condescend should prove the enormous extent of my control.

"Don't mind Oskar," Joanna said. "He's a blowhard. If you are having trouble at home, perhaps we could—"

"We've taken up enough of Queen Rani's time," Hannah interrupted with a sharp smile. "I'm sure Asmo has more people to introduce."

A wealth of nonverbal communication passed between Hannah and Asmo. I wished I had Valentin's ability to listen in on neural links, but by the time I considered asking him to link me in, Asmo was already directing me away.

"Oskar will be filling Valentin's ears by now," Asmo said. "Are you sure you won't be leaving tonight?"

"I'm sure," I said with careless confidence.

"Why?"

I eyed Asmo as if I were deciding whether or not to let him in on a secret. He grinned at me, a charming flash of white teeth that invited me to reveal everything. I gave him a truth hidden in a lie. "Valentin thinks I'm a damsel in distress who desperately needs his help. Now that I'm under his protection, he won't let anything happen to me. I just have to bide my time."

"Until what?"

I smiled and said nothing.

Asmo once again leaned in close. "Valentin isn't the only one with power," he confided with a smirk. "If you need help, I'm sure we can come to some sort of agreement." His hand slid a half centimeter lower, and I could practically feel Imogen's eagerness for it to drop just a fraction farther.

Unfortunately for her, while he bent the line to near breaking, he never *quite* crossed it.

———

VALENTIN RETURNED with two crystal flutes of sparkling wine. He held one of them out to me with an unreadable expression. "I brought you a drink, Queen Rani, as an apology for leaving."

I stepped away from Asmo and accepted the flute from Valentin with a genuine smile. I decided not to dwell on the happy little thrill I felt whenever he was near. He had been gone for less than half an hour, but it had felt like forever. "Thank you."

Valentin turned to Asmo. "Thank you, Advisor Copley, for keeping the queen company." The dismissal was impossible to miss.

Asmo ignored it.

"It was my pleasure, Your Majesty. Spending time with Samara is no hardship. She is enchanting." He lifted my free hand and kissed the backs of my fingers. When he lingered, I pulled my hand away, forcing him to release me. His eyes lit.

I hadn't been trying to entice him with a challenge, I'd just wanted my damn hand back. "Thank you for the escort," I said, keeping my tone polite.

"Have lunch with me tomorrow," he pressed.

"The queen is busy," Valentin said. "She will be lunching with me."

That was one way to throw down a gauntlet.

Asmo's expression turned sly. "How about breakfast, then?" he asked me. "I could cook for you."

He rubbed me the wrong way, but I had no real reason to turn him down. He might be a good source of information, and I'd done worse for less.

"Advisor Copley, I suggest you find someone else to breakfast with. Queen Rani is busy. If you will excuse us." Valentin didn't wait for an acknowledgement before he guided me away, his hand respectfully on my elbow.

I connected to Valentin via neural link. *If you were trying to discourage him, then it backfired spectacularly,* I said. *Asmo wants a challenge and you've just painted a target on me.*

Isn't that what someone who is under your thumb would do? he asked.

Who told you that?

Oskar. He wanted to banish you. When I refused, he told me why I should. You let Imogen put him on the ground?

Yes, because he threatened me. If my bodyguard let that go, she wouldn't be much of a guard. I paused, then forged on, concerned by his tone. *I warned you that I would say things to provoke them. And to be clear, I said you were enamored with me, not that you were under my thumb. But, either way, you know I didn't mean it, right? I wanted to see if your advisors would tell you or try to use it to their own advantage.*

I know, Valentin said, an odd note in his voice.

I stopped and turned to face him. "Are you sure?" I asked quietly.

His eyes searched mine. "I know," he repeated. Across the link, he continued, *You caught me off guard. So many people have lied to me...* His mental voice trailed off.

He'd been betrayed by those closest to him, and now I'd given him reason to doubt me. It had not been my smartest decision. *I'm sorry,* I said. *I was thoughtless. I will choose my strategies with more care in the future.*

Some of the tension drained from his face and he nodded. He offered me an arm and resumed walking once I'd taken it. *And you were right: I am enamored with you.* He didn't even give me time to process that bombshell before he continued, *Did you learn anything interesting?*

I blinked as I tried to get past the fact that he'd as much as admitted that his feelings went deeper than the simmering attraction between us. *You can't just say that and then carry on like nothing happened.*

Valentin grinned at whatever expression was on my face, but he didn't comment.

We will discuss that later. As for what I learned, I wish I had your ability. Hannah and Asmo had a moment I dearly would've loved to hear. Oskar told you what I said, despite the fact that he boasted he could make me disappear without your knowledge. Did any of your other advisors warn you?

No, Valentin said.

That could be a clue, or it could mean nothing. Traitors came in three varieties. The first wanted to watch the world burn and they didn't care who happened to be collateral damage. They were the easiest to catch because they almost universally acted in their own interest.

I doubted Valentin's traitors were that type or he would've caught them already.

The second variety wanted to affect some sort of change—like removing an Emperor they couldn't control. They didn't want to destroy the Kos Empire because then they would have to give up their cushy lives. They were harder to catch because they would do things that seemed loyal right before they stabbed you in the back.

The final variety of traitor was just in it for the money. They wouldn't much care who they hurt along the way, but they were shrewd and careful, so they were the most difficult to catch. They would make sure everything was in place before they stabbed you in the back and disappeared into the night. My former security specialist had fallen into this category.

My gut said Valentin's traitors fell into the second category. They didn't want to disrupt the status quo too much, but they'd much rather Valentin wasn't running the ship. Which meant they were likely working with Valentin's half-brother Nikolas.

Do you have any intel on where Nikolas is? I asked during a lull in the conversation.

No. He left before I returned from Arx and I haven't heard anything since. He has not answered any of my messages. My team tracked him for a week or so before they lost him. He was still in Koan during that time.

Is he allowed in the palace?

Yes. He's still my mother's son and my brother. Mother remains hopeful that he'll return soon.

I closed my eyes for a second against the urge to tell Valentin exactly how stupid that was. Now was not the time. Too bad there wasn't a convenient wall to bang my head against.

Valentin brought me the next best thing: the two advisors I hadn't yet alienated tonight. When Junior Mobb, the medical advisor, caught sight of me, his expression went carefully neutral. Even Myra's expression was less-than-welcoming.

Fantastic.

"Queen Rani, you remember Advisor Mobb and Advisor Shah, right?" Valentin asked.

"It's a pleasure to see you again," I said.

Myra looped her arm through Junior's and I had the sneaking suspicion that it was to keep him from darting off without acknowledging me. However, her expression remained guarded. "Are you enjoying your evening?" she asked.

Valentin thought Myra was loyal, but Junior was an unknown, so I went with a partial truth. "It's been interesting," I said.

"To be sure," she murmured.

I weighed my options, then initiated a connection with her via neural link. She met my eyes for several seconds before accepting.

What? Her tone was not welcoming.

You spoke to Oskar, I said.

I did. It was enlightening.

I made an executive decision. It might come back to bite me in the ass, but my gut said Myra wasn't the traitor, and I trusted my instincts. *Someone wants Valentin dead. I am not that person, but I'm going to find out who is.*

Her expression didn't even flicker. She didn't immediately respond, but she didn't close the link, either.

Valentin and Junior were talking about some new break-through medical research that Junior's team was working on. They were so engrossed that Myra and I just had to murmur in agreement.

You were testing him, she said at last. *And the rest of us. Why did I pass?*

I shrugged delicately. *You haven't. But I have to start somewhere, and I think you're loyal.*

Of course I'm loyal!

So says every traitor, right up until they betray you.

Myra inclined her head. *What can I do to help?*

You must have suspicions. Valentin's life is at risk. I need whatever information you have. And keep it to yourself that I'm looking.

I will consider it. She closed the link.

It was the best I could hope for. While it was a risk for me to trust her, it was a much bigger risk for her to trust me. For all she knew, I could be working for the traitors. And if things went poorly for me, I could leave for Arx at any time. She would be stuck here with the fallout from her actions.

As Myra's attitude warmed, Junior began including me in his

conversation with Valentin. Junior seemed especially sensitive to Myra's moods. He was happily married, and not to her, so I suspected that they were close friends.

Or they were silently communicating.

Junior had developed a new process for augmentation that cut down on the chance of rejection and also sped up the healing process. If trials continued to go well, it would be an incredible breakthrough.

"Junior's father performed my augmentation," Valentin said. "He is one of the greatest doctors of his time, and Junior is continuing to expand his research."

Junior smiled at the praise but waved his hand. "My father is a true genius. I just do what I can." He turned to me. "Do you have any augments, Queen Rani?"

"I do. I was augmented many years ago." I prayed he would leave it at that, but when his face lit with interest, I knew it wouldn't be so simple. His gaze ran down my body in a clinical assessment, but none of my augments were so obvious.

"Speed? Or perhaps strength?" he guessed.

Both, actually, but when I didn't immediately confirm or deny his guesses, Myra elbowed him. "It's not polite to speculate, Junior. You know that."

He ducked his head. "My apologies. Sometimes my curiosity overrides my manners. If you would like to share anything about your experience, my door is always open."

I doubted he wanted to hear that I'd gone to a brilliant black-market hack who had nearly killed me. The vast sum of money I'd spent had gotten me top-of-the-line augments, but none of the pre- or post-care that wealthy imperial citizens received. It'd taken me a month to recover and another six to retrain my muscle memory. I'd barely scraped by that year.

"I wish you luck with your trials," I said. "Improving the

process is good news for everyone." While I doubted it would bring the cost down to where normal people could afford casual augmentation, it was a step in the right direction.

Valentin touched my hand, a signal that we were about to depart, but before he could make excuses, the ballroom's double doors opened and a hush fell over the room.

A petite older woman in an exquisite dark gray gown entered. The uniformed attendant at the top of the stairs announced, "Her Imperial Majesty Dowager Empress Marguerite Kos of the Kos Empire."

It took a second for the statement to process through my stunned brain. Valentin's mother had just entered the ballroom.

8

Valentin tried to guide me toward his mother while I did my best to drag my feet without being obvious about it. I failed.

"What is wrong?" he asked.

"You didn't tell me your mother was here," I hissed under my breath.

He looked surprised. "Of course she's here. Where else would she be?"

The simple logic of the statement only made it worse. *Of course* she was here. I knew Valentin's mother still lived, and I knew she usually resided in Koan, but it had never occurred to me that she still attended official events. That was a research failure on my part.

Despite dragging my feet, Valentin had us positioned at the bottom of the stairs by the time the dowager empress had descended. I studied her from under my lashes.

Entertainment media through the years had led us to believe that empresses should be tall and stately, as sharp and beautiful as statues cut from icy crystal. Valentin's mother was none of those things. She was petite, plump, and pretty. Laugh lines fanned out from the corners of her eyes and her dark hair was threaded with gray. When she smiled at Valentin, her whole face lit up. She wore her emotions on her sleeve, something that had come through even in her photos.

Valentin kissed the air next to her cheek. "Hi, Mom."

"Hello, darling. Don't keep me in suspense; introduce me to the lovely lady on your arm."

"Mother, may I present Queen Samara Rani of the Rogue Coalition. Samara, this is my mother, Dowager Empress Marguerite Kos."

I bowed with the same level of deference I'd used for Valentin. "It is a pleasure to meet you, Your Majesty."

"Please, call me Margie. I'm so happy to meet you! I've heard so much about you." Her eyes sparkled with warmth. Clearly she hadn't heard the same rumors as everyone else. She lowered her voice. "Valentin told me how you saved him. You have my gratitude. If you ever need anything, you only have to ask."

"Thank you, Your M—Margie, but I'm afraid I did it for entirely selfish reasons. And Valentin has already more than repaid me."

Something sharp and fierce flashed across her face, totally at odds with her previous warm, easygoing attitude. "Saving your people isn't selfish," she chided. "And even if it were, you returned my son to me. That is priceless. My offer stands."

I bowed my head. "Of course. Thank you."

Valentin chuckled beside me. "You'll find that Mom gets her way more often than not," he confided. "She's tricky like that."

Margie smiled serenely and didn't deny the claim. She linked her arm through mine. "Let's take a turn around the room, see what the vultures are up to today. While we walk, tell me about your gorgeous dress. I'm always looking for a bright new tailor."

I told her about the tailor and the fittings and how my two best friends had bullied me into buying the dress despite the cost. That led to a discussion about my friends, and Arx, and much more than I'd been meaning to share. I caught myself mid-sentence. "Oh, you're good," I breathed.

Margie laughed, a light, joyful sound that turned heads, but her expression was shrewd. "For what it's worth, you caught on faster than most. I was empress for a long time. My husband was not an easy man, but I loved him fiercely. I found that I was the most help to him if people underestimated me, thought me a pretty bauble who loved to talk."

Questions crowded my tongue. If she had loved her husband, how did Nikolas end up Valentin's *half*-brother? And which brother did she support now? There was no polite way to ask, so I held my peace.

"Being underestimated is an excellent strategy," I agreed quietly. "And depending on the target, insultingly easy."

Margie's eyes danced with hidden amusement. "Indeed." She turned to Valentin. "I approve."

His expression didn't change, but he tensed slightly before darting a glance at me. When he found me watching him, a smile touched the corners of his mouth. I got the impression that I'd somehow passed a test I didn't know I was taking. He nodded to his mother.

"Tomorrow you will lunch with me," Margie told me. "Just the two of us. And your guard, of course." She softened the order with a bright smile.

"Mother—" Valentin started.

Margie patted his arm. "You can have her back after lunch." She nodded as if that settled it—and it did.

It was difficult to stay mad at Valentin for not warning me

about Margie when the lady herself was a familiar combination of charming and cunning. Now I knew where he got it.

A low, melodious chime announced dinner. Valentin escorted us both into the banquet hall. Luka, Imogen, and the dowager's guard trailed behind us. This room was just as impressive as the ballroom. A mixture of square and rectangular tables filled the space. Each was draped in a red or black tablecloth and laid with gleaming cutlery and sparkling stemware.

Valentin lead us to the far end of the banquet hall. A long table sat on a raised dais with chairs lining the far side, facing the room. A pristine white tablecloth hid the underside of the table. Imogen peeked under it before nodding her approval.

The table was laid with place settings for fifteen, with three obvious places of honor in the middle, denoted by ornate chairs. I hesitated to the call the center chair a *throne*, but it was far more elaborate than any of the chairs surrounding it.

When Valentin caught my raised eyebrow, he grinned sheepishly. "I may not be required to wear my full regalia to dinner, but some traditions are harder to get rid of than others."

Margie sat on Valentin's left and I sat on his right. My chair was surprisingly comfortable despite the ornamentation, with thick padding and armrests gently smoothed by many hands. When Imogen didn't sit down beside me, I turned to look for her.

She was far enough away that I linked to her. *Are you not eating?*

We have a table back here, she said. *Luka and I will take turns watching so the other can eat.* She caught my indignant expression and cut me off before I could protest. *It's not a big deal. As I said, I've guarded before. This is normal. Better, actually, because Luka says they feed us the same food your fancy ass gets.*

I smiled. She was finally loosening up, at least a little. *My fancy ass can keep watch for an hour. Make sure you eat.*

I will.

I closed the link and turned back to face forward. People were slowly trickling in, filling the tables in a haphazard order. Either seats were assigned or no one wanted to sit next to anyone else.

I checked our table, but there were no name cards. So when Oskar Krystopa pulled out the chair next to me, I had no warning. He scowled down at me before pulling out the next chair for his daughter.

Oh good, this would be a pleasant dinner. I mentally sighed and painted on a wide smile that made Oskar's scowl deepen.

The rest of the advisors took their seats. My side of the table included Oskar, his daughter, Junior, his husband, Myra, and finally an empty seat. My research had not been able to turn up any significant others in Myra's life and apparently she didn't feel inclined to bring a date to dinner.

I leaned forward and peeked at the other side of the table. Margie was on Valentin's left. The rest of that side included Hannah, her husband, Joanna, Joanna's date, Asmo, and finally a beautiful young woman who couldn't be more than nineteen. Asmo leaned over and nuzzled her while she giggled. My opinion of him sank lower.

With nothing else to do, I turned to Oskar. "We don't have to be enemies," I said quietly.

He responded with frosty silence.

Well, so much for diplomacy.

When most of the people had taken their seats, Valentin stood and pulled me up next to him. The sea of faces was no more welcoming than it had been when I'd been announced earlier.

A heavily muscled man stood at a table near the middle of the room. "Go home, Rogue bitch, and take your rebels with you! No one wants you here."

Valentin tensed beside me, but I placed a hand on his arm as excited murmurs swelled through the crowd. I waved Imogen back, then swept around the table. I stayed on the raised dais. I wanted everyone to have an excellent view of what was about to happen.

I gestured at him to join me. "Come and make me, my lord, if you think you can."

Uncertainty flashed across his face. I was a tiny woman in an evening gown, goading him into a fight. He was smart enough to smell a trap, but his pride wouldn't let him back down. Either that, or he was being paid to cause a scene.

He swaggered to the dais and jumped up, playing to the crowd. People were making bets, and most of them were against me. Some were betting that Valentin would get involved before the fight could start. I glanced back at him. His jaw was locked tight, his expression murderous.

I returned my attention to the man who'd insulted me. He was big and heavy, but he moved lightly, so he was augmented. I couldn't let my own pride be my downfall. I needed to make this short and brutal.

I crooked my finger at him and he rushed me. He threw a punch, fast, but I was faster. I grabbed his hand and twisted past him, using leverage on his arm joints and sheer strength to force him to the ground. I pinned him with my knee and pressed my plasma pistol to the back of his head.

He froze.

I leaned over him and quietly asked, "Did someone pay you to cause a scene?"

"I'm not telling you shit," he grumbled. I pulled his arm higher and he hissed out a breath but remained silent.

"I will break this arm, then I will break your other arm, and then I will start on your legs. Is whoever you're protecting worth that?" I jerked his arm up. Another centimeter and something would give, either the bone or the joint. "Who paid you?"

"I don't know," he gasped. "A woman approached me, knew I needed money. Offered me ten thousand credits to cause a scene, plus another ten thousand if I got you to leave. The money came from an anonymous account. That's all I know."

I linked Valentin. *Someone paid him. Once I let him up, I need you to have someone you trust detain him and get the details.*

Done, Valentin responded.

"Yield," I demanded, loud enough for the crowd to hear.

The man stayed stubbornly silent for a moment longer, then muttered, "I yield."

I let him up but didn't holster my pistol. An Imperial Guard escorted him from the room. I linked to Valentin. *How mad are you going to be about a plasma pulse hole in the ceiling? And this isn't some sort of heirloom cutlery, is it?*

Go ahead. And no.

I picked up a teaspoon from my place setting and sent it spinning into the air out over the crowd. I snapped the pistol up and fired a single shot. The teaspoon landed on a table, a neat hole punched dead center through the spoon's bowl.

A young woman at the table gasped, then held the spoon aloft. The room fell silent, and I looked around. "Would anyone else like to cause a scene?"

No one moved.

I resumed my place by Valentin, who turned his attention to the crowd. "I am delighted that Queen Rani has decided to grace us with her presence. She is my honored guest and a friend of the Kos Empire." His smile sharpened and he glared at the man who had insulted me. "Slights against her will be treated as slights against me." He turned to me, and I realized I was supposed to say something.

I stared out at the elites of the Kos Empire and wondered what I could say, if anything, that would bring them to my side after my little demonstration. "Thank you to Emperor Kos for inviting me to visit your beautiful city," I said. "I look forward to building on our existing treaty and strengthening our working relationship. That said, I will not tolerate any threats against myself, the Rogue Coalition, *or* Emperor Kos."

I didn't get a standing ovation—hell, I didn't even get a *sitting* ovation—but I hadn't expected one. No one else challenged me, so I called it a win.

"Enjoy your dinner," Valentin said. He sat. I sank down next to him.

Impressive shot, he linked.

Thank you. I've earned a lot of free drinks with that trick. I'll pay for the repair to your fancy ceiling.

Don't worry about it. It was worth it to watch you stun the entire court.

I wondered if I could shock any of his advisors to death by leaning over and kissing him. He must've caught the direction of my thoughts, because his expression heated.

The moment was broken when a discreet server placed a bowl of soup in front of Valentin. I masked my frustration behind a cool smile. Margie and I were served next, followed by the rest of the advisors and their guests.

Valentin tried to keep me entertained, but he kept getting drawn in by Hannah and talking to that side of the table. With no one to talk to, my thoughts turned back to this afternoon's attack.

I endured five courses, each more extravagant than the last, culminating in a spun sugar confection that should've been a delight, but everything tasted like ash. Someone wanted Valentin dead and me either dead or gone. And I was no closer to figuring out who.

I took a deep breath and reminded myself I'd been here for less than a day. Yes, that day had felt a hundred years long, but it was still just a day. I had time—at least a little.

———

By the time Valentin escorted me back to my suite, I was tired and grouchy. I'd been solidly ignored by Oskar and his daughter for the entire dinner, and trying to converse around them had been an exercise in frustration. I managed to meet Junior's husband, but only because I'd introduced myself after we'd finished eating.

Steven had been as amusing as Junior was serious. I'd liked him immediately and had relaxed for the first time in hours. Then Oskar had made a snide comment about conversing with the enemy and Steven had clammed up on me.

Afterwards, we had visited Werner Shipman, the man who had caused a scene at dinner. When he'd realized that he was in trouble with more than just me, he had decided to cooperate. Werner didn't have any handy vision or memory augments, but he'd worked with a sketch artist to create what he said was an accurate depiction of the woman who had approached him.

Neither Valentin nor Myra had recognized the woman, but I suggested that Valentin kick off an image matching process to compare the sketch to all known palace employees. If that didn't find any hits, he could expand it to run against a public database of Koan citizens.

Now we just had to wait.

I rubbed my eyes before remembering my eyeliner. My fingers came away smudged black. I had the irrational urge to punch something, but I settled for a heartfelt sigh.

We stopped in the foyer while Imogen swept the suite and

Luka pretended to give us privacy. Valentin touched my arm. "Are you okay?"

"It's been a long day."

"Do you want me to go?"

Now there was a dangerous question. I considered the wisdom of either choice for a few seconds. "No. Let's talk, just the two of us." I side-eyed Luka and lowered my voice. "I won't promise you more than that, but I'd like your company," I said candidly.

"Of course. Is it okay if I go change into more comfortable clothes?"

I smoothed the backs of my fingers down the lapel of his suit jacket. "I suppose. I'll miss the suit, though," I teased.

He grinned at me. "Conveniently, you'll get to see another one tomorrow. And the day after. And the day after that. I have an endless supply."

"In that case, go change and I'll do the same."

Valentin and Luka left just before Imogen returned. "You're good to go," she said.

"Thanks, and thanks for all of your help today. Take the rest of the night off. I'm not planning to go out again until in the morning. Valentin is coming over." At her sly grin, I clarified, "To *talk*."

"Well, you might want to wash your face. Just in case. I'm going to change and then go see if I can find a gym. I'll be gone an hour or two, but link me if something comes up. And don't go out without me."

"I wouldn't dream of it," I lied. At her skeptical expression, I relented a little. "I'll keep you apprised of my whereabouts."

She shook her head. "I deserve hazard pay just for keeping track of you," she grumbled good-naturedly.

"I'll see what Ari can do," I agreed with a smile.

We both retreated to our respective rooms. I carefully undressed and hung the dress in the wardrobe. Tomorrow, I would see if the palace staff could launder it for me. If they couldn't, hanging it would prevent the worst of the wrinkles.

I scrubbed my face free of makeup and put on a loose pair of lounge pants and a tank top with a built-in bra. This was me at my comfiest. If Valentin didn't run screaming from the room, it would be a good sign.

I carried my plasma pistol into the living room and set it on an end table. That way, if someone tried to come through the balcony, I'd be able to welcome them properly.

Imogen appeared, dressed in workout clothes. "I'm heading to the gym. I'll link you on my way back so I don't interrupt your *talk*." She narrowed her eyes. "And don't even think about leaving this suite without letting me know."

I huffed out an amused breath. "You're persistent, I'll give you that. Have a good workout."

"You, too," she said with an unrepentant grin.

She let herself out. For the first time today, I was alone in the suite with my thoughts, but all I could think about was Valentin's upcoming visit. Adrenaline set my nerves fluttering. I needed to calm the fuck down or I'd jump him as soon as he cleared the door.

And I was pretty sure he would let me.

Not helping.

I closed my eyes and willed myself to focus. Because despite what my body thought, I really did need to talk to Valentin.

My nerves refused to settle. I laughed at myself and went to look for a drink.

9

The suite's kitchenette came with a fully stocked bar. I was perusing the options when the doorbell rang. I firmly ordered the butterflies in my stomach to take a hike. Two deep breaths and I'd pulled myself back into a semblance of calm and controlled.

That control wavered precariously when I checked the door display. Valentin was in a tight, black T-shirt that hugged the muscles in his chest and a loose pair of charcoal-gray lounge pants. He was barefoot.

I closed my eyes against a wave of desire mingled with unexpected bashfulness. Just because I was confident and happy with my body didn't mean I was blind. Even on my best day, I wasn't in his league.

I swung open the door before self-doubt could plague me. He was here because he wanted to be, and that was enough.

A slow smile spread across his face. "Hi."

I couldn't stop my answering smile. "Hi." I stepped back. "Come in. Imogen went to find the gym. You have a gym somewhere, right?"

His eyebrows rose. "Yeah. In fact, Luka was heading there. Think I should warn him?"

We shared a conspiratorial grin.

I led Valentin back to the kitchenette. "I was just contemplating a drink," I said. "Can I get you something?"

"I'll have what you're having."

"Adventurous, since I don't know what I'm having yet."

"I trust you." He said it quietly, but it had a ring of truth—and felt deeper than just our talk about drinks.

I studied the bottles as if my survival depended on it. Valentin's staff had outdone themselves. Every liquor was a high-end brand that was difficult to find and incredibly expensive. I pulled out a whisky that routinely went for more than fifty credits a serving.

When I held it up, Valentin nodded his acceptance. I poured us each a couple fingers, neat, and handed him his glass. I lifted my own and breathed in the woodsy, smoky scent mixed with the sharp bite of alcohol.

"To us," Valentin toasted simply.

"To us," I echoed. I took a sip. Warm fire rolled down my throat and settled in my belly. I hummed my appreciation. This was a damn fine whisky.

Valentin cleared his throat. "Shall we?" he asked with a wave toward the living room.

I moved to the sofa and sat with my back against one of the armrests. Valentin sat in the middle, close enough that I could reach out and touch him, but far enough away to be respectable. I tucked my bare toes under his thigh, then smiled at him. "You can keep my feet warm."

He held his free hand to his heart. "It would be my honor," he said solemnly, but his eyes danced with merriment.

A playful Valentin was nearly irresistible. I could just crawl over there and—I cut off that line of thinking. I savored another sip of whisky while I decided on an opening gambit. I needed to know more about his advisors, but I was also desperately curious about his mother.

Valentin made the decision for me. "Myra told me that you asked her for help."

"I did. It might be a mistake, but I need an ally who isn't the emperor. My gut says she's loyal, but even if she's not, it will give me more information than I have now. Tell me what you think about the attack."

"You tell me. You don't have any preconceptions, and I don't want to influence you."

"They operated more like a military unit than a mercenary unit. They obviously have access to a lot of high-powered weapons and good information. If the sweep of the folly happened, then they're well trained and fast. If I had to guess with what I know right now, I'd say it's a squad of Quint soldiers trying to look like mercenaries."

Valentin remained quiet, so I kept going. "Motivation is murkier. Nikolas obviously wants to be emperor, and some of your advisors back him because they worked deals with him for years. But, by all accounts, you're a *good* emperor. It can't all be ideological. There has to be a great deal of money on the line."

"I am working with Quint Chairwoman Soteras on a treaty to end the war," Valentin said softly.

I sucked in a breath. "How many people know about it?"

"My advisors. Chairwoman Soteras and her council."

"Damn. No wonder half of the universe wants you dead." War was a very lucrative business as long as you didn't have to actually dirty your hands with the fighting and dying.

Money was at the heart of the ongoing war between Quint and Kos. They both claimed a series of rare, easily habitable planets.

Terraforming was expensive and time-consuming. Planets where people could live with minimal changes were in short supply and both sides needed the room for expansion.

They couched it in other terms, of course, because an ideological war was more popular than a mercenary one—*the enemy is trying to destroy our way of life!* And to a certain degree, that was true. Quint citizens didn't think an emperor was fit to rule, and Kos citizens didn't think Quint's corrupt sham of a democracy actually looked out for the people it was supposed to protect. Both were right, and wrong.

The Rogue Coalition had a pony in this race, too, because the end of the war—the true end, not some farce—would likely mean the end of our little band of misfits. Without the threat of war, people could return to their former homes and rebuild their lives. It was a bittersweet thought.

"Who's pushing back the hardest?" I asked.

"Oskar, Hannah, and Asmo." Military strategy, diplomatic relations, and domestic affairs.

Oskar made sense—military strategy would lose significant importance once the war was over. Hannah should be happy, though, because diplomatic relations would reopen with Quint, increasing her value. Asmo's domestic affairs position was more of a mixed bag. The end of the war would be good for the majority of the Kos Empire, except for those in positions of wealth and power.

"Do they have good reasons?" I asked.

"Oskar remembers the last treaty. Quint signed it with no intention of honoring it. They used it as a short break to build up their military before attacking once again."

I frowned at him. "I believe they learned that maneuver from your father. And possibly Oskar himself."

"Yes, we are not blameless," Valentin said grimly. "I'm trying to change that."

"What about Hannah and Asmo?"

"They both think that we would be better off destroying Quint entirely, despite the fact that we have not managed it in the last thirty years. They refuse to believe that a treaty will solve anything."

"That's a little bloodthirsty for someone supposedly in charge of diplomatic relations. No wonder you've been at war for so long."

"Bloodthirsty might be an understatement," Valentin muttered. "I think if it were up to her, we'd fight them to our dying breath."

I filed that information away. "Is anyone in favor?"

"Junior and Myra are both in favor. Junior wants better access to Quint medical research and Myra thinks I'll be safer if Quint isn't out for my blood."

"Speaking of that, have you heard anything about Commander Adams?" Quint commander Tony Adams had attacked Arx because I'd rescued Valentin from him. When Adams was defeated by Valentin's forces, he'd escaped in a shuttle and disappeared. It'd been weeks and he still hadn't reappeared. I hoped he was dead, but I wasn't holding my breath.

Valentin glanced away. "My people in Iona heard rumors that he briefly returned to the city last week, but they were never able to get confirmation."

Iona was Quint Confederacy's capital city on Casseda Prime. It didn't surprise me that Valentin had people there. Just as I wouldn't be surprised if I learned that Quint had people in Koan.

"He could throw a wrench in any peace talks, especially if Chairwoman Soteras values his input. He didn't seem amenable to peace."

"Adams is against any sort of peace that doesn't involve our complete surrender." Valentin grimaced and continued, "As for whether he can influence the chairwoman, it may not matter. Earlier today, my intelligence staff intercepted a message that indicated Adams was headed for—or possibly in—Koan. That's why I was pulled away this afternoon."

My pulse sped up. If I'd known Adams was here, I could've been looking for him. Instead, Valentin had kept me in the dark. "Why did you wait to tell me?" I demanded.

Valentin remained calm. "I was waiting for confirmation that the message was legitimate and not a trap. A second message was intercepted this evening during dinner. The information is legitimate, but it may still be a trap."

"Is Adams behind the attack this afternoon? Is he working with one of your advisors?"

"I don't know." Valentin blew out a frustrated breath. "The messages didn't have any additional information. Hell, one of my advisors could be faking them, but if so, they're far better than anything I've seen before. I just don't know. You now have all of the information I have." There was no reproof in his tone despite the fact that I'd snapped at him.

I took a sip of whisky and let the slow burn remind me to be patient. Valentin had promised to try to be more open with information, but people didn't change immediately and breaking a life-long habit was *hard*. And Koan was a city of twenty million people. Even if Valentin had told me about Adams earlier, I wouldn't have found him today.

I slid around so I was sitting on my heels next to Valentin. It put us at eye level. "I'm sorry I was short with you," I said. "Thank you for sharing your intelligence. If you find anything else, I would appreciate being looped in."

"Of course. I planned to tell you that Adams was here as soon as I knew the information was good." He clinked his glass against mine and grinned. "We're partners, after all."

Warmth that had nothing to do with alcohol and everything to do with affection spread through my chest. Not only did I find him smart and sexy as hell, but I also *liked* Valentin, quite a lot. I liked his cool calm. I liked how he respected me, and listened to me, and didn't underestimate me. I liked the way looked at me like I was the most beautiful woman in the room. I especially liked it when he called us partners. I set my glass on the nearby table. "I'm going to kiss you now."

His answering grin was filled with wicked heat. "Please do."

I leaned forward but I could already tell the angle was going to be wrong, so I pressed a kiss to his cheek.

"Not exactly what I had in mind," he teased, "but I'll take—"

His sentence ended on a groan as I swung myself into his lap, my legs straddling his. I sucked in a breath when I realized exactly how thin the layers of fabric between us really were. I was walking a dangerous, dangerous line. "Is this okay?" I asked.

"Yes, but you still owe me a kiss," he murmured. He gripped my hips and pulled me closer. The movement sent shivers of pleasure dancing through my system. He made a low, pleased sound, and his hands flexed but remained where they were.

I leaned forward and pressed my lips to his. I kept the kiss light, exploring, building the tension. Valentin let me until I licked into his mouth. Then he buried a hand in my hair, tilted my head, and kissed me long and deep. By the time we came up for air, he was fully aroused and it was all I could do to stay still and not mindlessly rock against him.

He pressed a kiss to the corner of my mouth, then nuzzled my jaw, slowing the pace. "You are amazing," he whispered against my skin.

I chuckled. "I'm no closer to figuring out who wants you dead, and then I yelled at you because you didn't give me unverified data. I am not amazing."

"You've got my advisors running scared *and* you impressed my mother. In less than a day. You. Are. Amazing." Each word was punctuated with a teasing kiss on my neck.

"Keep going and maybe I'll agree with you." I tilted my head, giving him better access. I felt him smile before he obliged. He bit me gently and my arousal spiked.

I slid my hand to the back of his head. His dark hair was short and soft, and I played with it for a moment before I pulled his head up to mine. "You're pretty amazing yourself," I murmured against his mouth.

His eyes crinkled as he grinned, then he parroted my words back to me. "I'm no closer to figuring out who wants me dead. And I didn't immediately share important information. I'm not amazing."

I wasn't always the best about sharing my feelings, but here, couched in the safety of a game, I told Valentin the truth. "You helped catch two of our attackers *and* you trusted me to handle myself with your advisors." I kissed him. "You." Another kiss. "Are." I nibbled on his lower lip. "Amazing."

His smile promised wicked, wicked things. "Keep going."

I tugged on the bottom of his shirt. He leaned away from the sofa and pulled it over his head, revealing golden skin stretched over taut muscles. I shivered as I ran my hands across the hard planes of his chest.

"You are perfect," I whispered. I kissed him and his mouth parted beneath mine. I rocked against him as the kiss deepened. He was hot and hard under me and I wished our clothes were gone.

He pushed up my shirt. The built-in bra stumped him for a second, but then he pulled the stretchy elastic up, revealing my breasts. At his urging, I pulled the shirt the rest of the way off. He leaned back to look, and I felt his groan everywhere we touched.

"You are so beautiful." He whispered it like a prayer, then his hot mouth closed over my nipple and my brain short-circuited. I rolled my hips, grinding against him like I was a teenager making out for the first time. It wasn't enough.

Pants, we needed to remove these pants.

I leaned back, planning to ask him if he wanted to do just that, when *Invictia* blared a proximity warning to me via neural link. I froze and Valentin picked up on my distraction. "What's wrong?"

"Someone is near my ship." I blinked, trying to focus through the desire to ignore whatever it was and go right back to what we were doing.

"Imogen?"

"No, she wouldn't set off an alarm." I frowned and connected to the ship's systems, trying to get a visual. The warning came from the rear of the ship, but the cameras had limited visibility in that area and showed nothing out of place.

"I'm sending a security patrol to check it out," Valentin said.

"Thank you," I murmured, still trying to find a camera angle that showed me what the ship was sensing. It had picked up at least two people behind the ship, but I couldn't activate the defensive measures without knowing who it was. I didn't want to be responsible for murdering a couple of curious kids.

Less than a minute later, an attack warning screamed across the link, then cut off halfway through when my connection to the ship went dead. What the hell was happening? I caught a flash of light and heard a distant *boom* as something large exploded in the distance.

Dread churned in my gut as I unsuccessfully tried to reconnect with my ship.

"That came from the direction of the spaceport," Valentin said with alarm. His expression went distant, then his face drained of color. He glanced at me, stricken.

With a sinking heart, I already knew what he was going to say.

"Your ship was attacked. Fire crews are on their way, but it doesn't look good. Based on the snippet of video I saw, it looks like a total loss."

10

Invictia had been my home for more than a decade, and now she was burning like a miniature sun, despite the best efforts of the fire crews. Honestly, even if they put the fire out, Valentin was right—the ship was a total loss.

The attackers had gone for the more lightly shielded engine propulsion nozzle. They had set the heavy, shaped explosive in such a way that it blew open the ship's stardrive, which in turn took half the ship with it.

Invictia would never fly again. My home was lost. *I* was lost.

I donned my shirt with numb fingers. I'd moved many of my mementos into Arx after the first couple of years, when I'd really started putting down roots, but *Invictia* herself was my most treasured possession.

It felt like just yesterday when I'd stepped on board for the first time. When I'd looked around at what a decade of constant bloodshed had earned—a chance to change, to make my own choices, to live my own life.

Invictia was not only my home, she was the first step I'd taken toward freedom. The ship represented every good thing I'd ever had in my life, and now she was burning, and there wasn't a fucking thing I could do to stop it.

The loss *hurt,* a knife-sharp pain that burrowed into my chest and stole my breath. My eyes were hot and dry. The tears would come once the shock wore off, once vengeance was mine.

And vengeance would be mine, but for now, the grief drowned out everything else.

Valentin prevented me from running blindly into a trap by patching the security feed through to the suite's main screen, so I could watch as *Invictia* slowly succumbed to flames from the safety of the suite. But the distance didn't lessen the pain.

Valentin wrapped his arms around me in a gentle hug. I laid my head against his chest and tried not to think about how when I'd reached for something I'd desired for myself, I'd lost the most important thing in my life. I wanted to rail against the unfairness of the universe.

Bitter tears flooded my eyes, but I blinked them away. I couldn't start crying, not yet.

An urgent neural link came from Imogen. When I answered, she demanded, *Are you okay? Where are you?*

I'm in my suite. Valentin is here as well.

Stay there. I'm on my way. Samara, I... I'm so sorry.

I closed the link and blinked away more tears. Sorrow would get me nowhere and rage would burn down the world. I grasped at control, then pushed away from Valentin's comforting presence. "Who is responsible?"

For all that he'd been gently comforting me, one glance at him revealed that Valentin was beyond furious. His jaw was clenched and his eyes blazed with fury. The distance in his gaze meant he was also sending orders via neural link. "The attackers were not caught," he growled, "but it was a team of two. I have the video."

A second window appeared on screen. *Invictia* glowed

greenish gray in the night vision video. Two people, likely men from their builds, came in from the left, pushing a cargo sled covered with a tarp. Both wore spaceport staff uniforms with hats pulled low. Only their jawlines were visible.

It took them less than a minute to attach the explosive device. Then they just strolled away. I watched until the bright blast of the explosion took out the camera. Fury, bright and blinding, tried to overwhelm my control. I funneled it into resolve. I would catch these fuckers, and I would make them pay.

And my vengeance would be swift and brutal.

I took a steadying breath. "I'm assuming those weren't really spaceport workers?"

"No. If I had to guess, I would say they were part of the same squad that attacked us this afternoon. I've got a team trying to track their location."

I didn't expect them to have much luck. I knew from experience that it was all too easy to hide in a city this big. "Why attack my ship? They had to know I wasn't on it. Unless they wanted me grounded and unable to leave quickly."

Valentin sighed. "Someone is trying to undermine you and our agreement. I have no doubt that in a few minutes, gossip circles will be buzzing about the attack from Rogue Coalition rebels. I'll be pressured to distance myself from an unstable foreign government. Anything you say will be considered unreliable and self-serving. I'm sorry I dragged you into this."

I stopped in front of where he was leaning against the sofa and tried to dredge up some of my earlier playfulness to break the tension. "I can work with unreliable and self-serving. But you owe me a new ship." It came out far wobblier than I wanted, and I bit my lip.

He carefully drew me in until I rested against his chest again, then wrapped his arms around me. "Let me know what you want and I'll make it happen," he promised softly. He blew out a breath that ruffled my hair, then quietly continued, "I'm so fucking sorry, Samara. You lost your home because of me. This is my fault, and I know I can't ever fix it, but I'm going to try. Whatever you need, I will do it."

I'd been joking, trying to lighten the mood with an obviously outrageous request. His abrupt agreement threw me, as did his attempt to take all of the blame. I pulled back far enough to stare at him. "You can't buy me a ship. This wasn't your fault. This was the fault of whoever attacked. And I plan to make them regret their life choices."

"I can and will buy you a new ship. Yours was destroyed because of a security failure on my part. I might not have ordered the attack, but I offered you my protection when you agreed to come to Koan. That protection failed. I know what *Invictia* meant to you, and I can never replace what you lost, but I can give you the next best thing."

"Valentin, you can't give me a ship."

He smiled at me, the first I'd seen since the attack. "If you don't pick something, I'll pick for you."

"I'm going to pick something hideously expensive. You should back out now, while you have a chance."

"Your pitiful attempt to bankrupt me is noted," he said with a derisive sniff, nose in the air. He broke into a grin and brushed his fingers over my jaw. "Do your worst."

A brief knock sounded before the door opened, revealing Imogen and Luka. Both still wore their workout gear. It was eerie to watch them both check us, then check the room for threats in a very similar fashion. I reluctantly stepped away from Valentin.

Finally, Imogen's gaze returned to me. "What happened?"

I kept a tight rein on my emotions, but my voice still came out in a furious growl. "Someone blew up my ship."

"Was anyone hurt?"

I felt a stab of shame as I realized I'd been so wrapped up in my own pain and fury that I hadn't asked about anyone else.

"No," Valentin said. "It was a targeted strike against Samara's ship and nothing else. The nearby ships took only minor damage to their hull shielding."

"Same attackers?" Luka asked.

Valentin shrugged. "I think so, but I wasn't able to catch either of them. We have video, but their faces are obscured."

"They're trying to divide you," Imogen said. "To sow doubt and discredit Samara."

Valentin nodded in agreement. "Rumors are powerful. Stopping them will prove difficult."

A quick mental check of the local news net proved exactly how true that was. The rumors were already spreading. And the attack details were spot on, with the exception of the perpetrators. Someone with access to the security footage had leaked the information.

I sighed and decided. "We don't need to stop the rumors. I'm going to embrace them. Behold your new refugee Rogue Queen, desperate to hold onto the power that is slipping away into the hands of rebels."

"It's dangerous. You'll be seen as weak and vulnerable. My court will do their best to eat you alive."

"Let them try," I said with absolute confidence, both in myself and in him. I knew that as long as Valentin breathed, he would do everything in his power to protect me from his court. I just had to keep him breathing.

"Are you sure it *isn't* Rogue rebels?" Luka asked.

I was, but it was a valid question for him to ask, especially with the new rumors flying around. Just because they'd had trouble before I arrived didn't mean that I hadn't brought my own trouble with me.

Before I could answer, Imogen rolled her eyes. "She's sure. She's too modest to say so, but she inspires loyalty in all of us."

Luka slanted a glance at her. "You're hardly an impartial judge."

She bristled at him, but I cut in, "He's right to ask the question, Imogen."

"I contacted Ari earlier," she said. "Everything is fine in Arx and she laughed at the thought of rebels. As she pointed out, why would people rebel now that we have food and jobs again, all thanks to our queen? There is no rebellion. Rogue citizens are fiercely protective of Samara and happy with her leadership."

"People rebel for many reasons," Luka said. "And your people have the necessary skill."

"Many of my people do have the skills," I agreed. "But killing me won't automatically give someone else control. The people made me queen. They will only follow someone they choose, and no one on my advisory council wants the job. Without an obvious replacement, the Rogue Coalition will fracture upon my death, something Quint would be all-too-happy to exploit."

"Perhaps you should look to your own people," Imogen said to Luka.

"We are," he agreed easily.

"I don't think it's a coincidence that intel indicated Commander Adams was in Koan right before the attacks ramped up. These attacks have seemed more military than mercenary to me, and Commander Adams has a grudge against both of us."

Valentin inclined his head in agreement. "Do you have a plan?"

"We're fighting on two fronts," I said. "We have an unknown team of attackers, likely Quint soldiers, and they want one or both of us dead. We also have an unknown number of your advisors who may or may not be working with that team."

"That would've been good information to have earlier," Imogen growled.

"It wasn't my secret to share, but now the attackers have upped the stakes. There are too many unknowns. Tonight I'm going to work on the attack team. Tomorrow I'll keep working on the advisors."

"What can I do?" Valentin asked.

"You can stay here and act normal. I'm going to do some research on Koan, then go check a few local watering holes, see if any new teams have popped up in the last week or so."

My statement was met with two immediate denials from Imogen and Valentin and one skeptically arched brow from Luka. Good to know that I inspired confidence.

"Did you forget who I am?" I asked, my voice soft with menace. "I was not born a princess. I did not grow up in an ivory tower. Blood and death were my profession for years before I became queen. I can handle myself with a few mercenaries and when I find the team who attacked *Invictia*—and I *will* find them— I am going to make an example of them that no one will soon forget. Cross the Rogue Queen at your peril."

Those fuckers had destroyed my *home*. There was no escape for them, nowhere they could hide. I would find them and shatter everything they held dear.

And I would enjoy every second of it.

In fact, after the day that I'd had, I looked forward to teaching a very memorable lesson to the first person who tried to screw with me. I knew going out alone was dangerous, but I couldn't take Imogen. She was a good soldier and a phenomenal body-guard, but she'd never been a mercenary or a thief or anyone else on the shady side of the law. She would be marked as a cop—at best—in two seconds flat.

"Just because we're worried for you doesn't mean we don't respect your skills," Valentin argued quietly.

I sighed and rubbed my face. Rage and pain pulsed under my skin, making me twitchy and overly sensitive. "I know; I'm sorry. But I can't just sit here and do nothing. I *can't*."

"I will go with you," Valentin said.

"You have the most recognizable face in the city. You can't go with me, though I appreciate the offer."

"I will go in his place," Luka said.

"Like hell you will," Imogen countered. "For all I know, you're in on it and will stab Samara in the back as soon as you're out of my sight."

I knew Valentin trusted Luka with his life, but I was kind of with Imogen on this one. The big, taciturn guard didn't seem to care much for me, and it would certainly eliminate some danger for Valentin if I were to disappear.

Luka shrugged. "Then I will go alone."

"No, I'm going, one way or another. How well do you know the typical merc hangouts? And, more importantly, how well do they know you?" I asked.

"You can't be seriously—" Imogen started, but she bit off the rest of the sentence when I sent her a warning look.

"I know them well. And as far as they know, I'm a personal security specialist."

I waved at his ice blond hair and solidly muscled frame. "You're not exactly inconspicuous. Why hasn't anyone pegged you as Valentin's guard?"

"I don't go often, and I know how to stay under the radar."

I stared at Luka while I weighed my options. He waited patiently and didn't so much as shift in annoyance. Having a guide would make things faster, but if he wanted to lead me into a trap, I was presenting him with a golden opportunity. And while I could send him on his own, my name might open more doors than his.

Imogen linked me. *I vehemently object to this plan,* she said without preamble.

Your objection is noted.

Samara, I know you are hurting right now, but don't rush into danger without reason. I raised a cool eyebrow at her and she flushed but didn't back down. *It's my job to save you from yourself.*

"You may not trust him, but trust me," Valentin said at last. "Luka will keep his word. If he promises to keep you safe, he will."

"He owes me nothing."

"No, but I owe Valentin everything," Luka said. "I will keep you safe, for him."

"Who will look after you while Luka is gone?" I asked Valentin.

"I have other guards," he said, "but it might be better to keep this quiet. I could stay here with Ms. Weber, if she doesn't mind."

I mind, Imogen said across the link, but she didn't protest aloud.

"We need to make a public announcement, to assure everyone that I am still very much alive. Then I need an hour before we leave," I said.

"I will go change," Valentin said. "Link me when you're ready to make the announcement. We'll use my office."

As he left, I couldn't help but wish this night had ended differently.

───────

"I WILL GO with Luka while you stay here," Imogen tried for the sixth time. We'd gone around in circles for the last hour and a half, both before and after Valentin and I had made our announcement. Now I was putting the finishing touches on my fourth outfit of the evening and she was still trying.

When an unexpected link came through from Ari, I sighed in exasperation. "Really? You snitched on me to Ari?"

"Maybe she saw the news on the feed." When I just stared, Imogen relented. "She told me to keep her informed."

I rolled my eyes at her and accepted the link. *Hello, Ari. Is everything okay?*

You tell me, she growled. *Did your best friend's ship just blow up without a word from said friend that she was okay?*

Ouch. I deserved that one. *Sorry. If it makes you feel better, I wasn't anywhere near the ship when it blew up.*

I already got a full report from Imogen. You're going to give her an aneurysm.

You know I can't send her into the underbelly of Koan.

Ari sighed across the link. *I know. Are you sure about this?*

Yes.

Then be careful. Keep me posted. And remember that Stella will kick your ass if you get hurt again.

I will be careful. I'm taking Valentin's guard Luka for backup.

She was silent for a long moment. *Watch him. He's sharper than he looks.*

I will. How are things in Arx? No mutinies happening while I'm gone?

She chuckled. *No. But Zita and Eddie are in a heated battle to see who can produce the most delicious pastry. I've got twenty credits on Eddie. I think he's a dark horse.*

Eddie ran the mess hall in Arx and Zita ran the bakery. Eddie was gifted, but Zita had years of experience on him. *I hope you're ready to lose your money.*

Ten credits say I don't, she promptly replied.

Done, but don't tell Eddie or Zita. I don't want to eat burnt food when I come home.

Your secret is safe with me. We're all staying mum, and they're pretending they don't know about the betting, Ari said. She paused and her tone turned serious. *Do you want me to send another ship?*

Do we have one we can spare? We had a few fighters and a massive city ship, but the Rogue Coalition wasn't exactly flush with extra ships capable of tunneling to Koan.

I'll find something and have it delivered to the main spaceport under a false name, so they don't blow it up before you get a chance to see it. I'll let you know when it arrives. Be careful. I mean it, Samara.

Thank you. I will be. You be careful, too. Someone went to a lot of trouble to ensure I can't quickly return to Arx. They could be planning to hit you next.

I will increase patrols, she said. *And Valentin still has ships in the sector. We'll be okay.*

Good. Take care.

We said our good-byes and cut the link.

"Ari thinks I'm going to give you an aneurysm," I told Imogen.

"She's right," she muttered not quite under her breath.

"Would you prefer to return to Arx? No one will hold it against you. Exploding ships are far beyond what you signed up for."

"I wouldn't be much of a bodyguard if I bailed at the first sign of adversity," Imogen said. "I'm staying. But I still think I should go out in your place."

I smiled at her tenacity. "We'll have to agree to disagree."

"Be careful. Promise me you won't ditch Luka. He might not have the best manners, but he's strong and fast."

Her tone of voice made the sentiment as much warning as endorsement.

"I don't plan on leaving him behind. And I will be careful."

11

I left Imogen in the suite and met Luka near Valentin's room. Valentin had decided to stay in his own suite. Twenty credits said Luka had persuaded him that Imogen couldn't be trusted to watch his back.

Luka looked over my outfit with a critical eye. I had on nondescript black utility pants, heavy boots, and a long-sleeved, stretchy black shirt. A sturdy gray jacket covered me past my hips, and a cap pulled low obscured my face. A thin scarf wrapped around my neck up to my chin, leaving just my jaw and mouth fully visible. All of the items were of good quality but well worn.

I had short knives in both boots and a plasma pistol in a shoulder holster. The belt around my waist held spare magazines as well as my long combat knife. I was armed enough to give someone pause before attacking me.

Luka was dressed similarly to me, minus the coat. He wore his plasma pistol openly in a belt holster. He looked huge and intimidating, which wasn't a bad look when hitting up mercenary hangouts.

"Ready?" I asked.

"Are you sure you want to go?"

"Where is our first stop?"

"I planned to hit Blind, BlackHeart, and Jack's."

He'd named the top three places I'd found during my research. At least he wasn't leading me astray from the very beginning. "Sounds good. I propose we split up and enter separately when we get there. We can gather twice as much information."

"Can you handle yourself?"

My smile was not friendly. "I can only hope someone decides to find out."

Luka decided not to be that someone. Smart man.

We exited the palace through an underground tunnel. Once out, we caught a public transport that carried us from the clean, shiny Imperial Garden, through the towering business districts, and out into the run-down industrial fringes of the city. The buildings got lower, dirtier, and darker.

It was getting close to midnight local time, but the streets still teemed with people. A city this large never fully slept, and for many of the people of this neighborhood, their day was just beginning.

The transport stopped in a shadowed alley two blocks from the bar. Luka stepped out first, scanned the area, and then moved aside to let me exit. The night air was a pleasant enough temperature, but the alley stank of old urine and rotting garbage.

"Last chance to back out," he said.

"Circle the block so you come from another direction and wait at least five minutes. In the unlikely event that the bar is full of Quint soldiers wanting my head, I'll link you so you can join in the fun."

"I will watch until you make the door. Then you are on your own."

"See you inside."

I walked out of the alley with the purposeful stride and easy confidence of someone who knew exactly where she was going, and thanks to my link to the net and prior research, I did. Blind wasn't much to look at, just a generic black door in a low-slung plascrete building. No bouncer, no sign, no windows.

Hesitation would get me pegged as an easy mark, so I pulled open the door and strolled inside as if I'd been coming here for years. The interior of the bar was pitch black, but my night-vision contact lenses adjusted quickly enough to show me the man reaching for me from my left.

I dodged his grab and pulled my knife. He backed off, hands up. "Easy, darling, I don't want any trouble. Just making sure you're in the right place."

Right. The greenish gray output of my lenses was good enough to see that he was dressed in dark clothes and built like a tank. One of these days I was going to have to buy higher quality lenses so I could see in color, but I wasn't used to having money again.

A quick glance showed a typical interior. A long bar spanned the back wall and high tables with barstools were situated throughout the room. The crowd was thick enough that nearly all of the tables were full and people stood clumped together in little groups. Music played, just loud enough to cover quiet conversation.

The man backed off farther when I didn't sheathe my knife. "Feisty little thing, aren't you?" he asked from the false safety of a two-meter distance.

I bared my teeth at him. "Come closer and find out."

He chuckled and the tension in the room broke. "How about I buy you a drink instead?"

Based on the way the others in the bar were stealthily attempting to eavesdrop on our conversation, this man was important. I sheathed my knife in a show of goodwill. "I never turn down free beer."

"A beer for the lady!" the man shouted to the bartender. He held out a hand. "I'm Finlay and this is my bar. Welcome to Blind."

I warily shook his hand. His massive paw dwarfed mine, but his grip was firm, not overpowering. Finlay was perhaps two decades older than my own thirty, but time had treated him kindly. His hair was a lighter color, perhaps a light brown or auburn, but I couldn't quite tell thanks to the night-vision lenses. Laugh lines fanned out from the corners of his eyes, and he had a ready smile. He waved for me to follow him and forged a path through the mingling crowd.

We were nearly to the bar when someone grabbed my ass. I caught their wrist and spun around, knife out. A drunk man blinked blearily at me. He was young, early twenties, but the alcohol had stolen any beauty he'd possessed.

"Do you like this hand?" I asked. For emphasis, I tapped it with the flat of my blade.

"No need to be hasty," Finlay said from over my shoulder. "Wade didn't mean any harm. Did you, Wade?"

"No?" It came out a question as Wade tried to focus on Finlay. He should've been cut off several drinks ago.

"Apologize to the lady."

"Sorry, lady," Wade said. He clearly had no idea what he was apologizing for.

"Keep your hands to yourself unless you want to lose them," I advised. When he just blinked at me, I sighed and let him go.

"Thank you," Finlay murmured when I rejoined him. "Wade's working through some stuff. Not a bad kid, but not too bright right now."

At the bar, Finlay jerked his head at the two people sitting at the end, and they grumbled but gave up their seats. He let me pick my seat and I chose the one where I could sit with my back to the wall. The bartender poured two glasses of dark beer and set them in front of us.

I raised my glass. "Cheers."

Finlay echoed the toast and took a long drink. I sipped my own beer. After the whisky earlier, I needed to pace myself.

"So what brings you to Koan?" Finlay asked.

"Business."

"You wouldn't have anything to do with that little fireworks show earlier, would you?" His tone was decidedly less friendly.

"No." I didn't elaborate, but I didn't pretend ignorance, either. The local net was wild with speculation about who could've been behind the attack.

"Good."

"Does anyone know who's responsible?" I asked. When he slanted a sharp glance at me, I shrugged. "Gotta make money somewhere, and I've got some free time on my hands."

"Every hunter in the city is going to be after the Rogue rebels. If they're smart, they've cleared out."

Evidently that rumor wasn't going to die on its own.

The door opened and Luka stepped inside, followed by a slightly shorter man in a long, deeply hooded coat that obscured his face. The new bouncer didn't bother to approach them. Luka swept his gaze around the room without stopping on me, but I was positive he knew exactly where I was.

Luka made his way to the bar, and the other man disappeared into the crowd, his movement oddly familiar. The build was right. I narrowed my eyes. Surely Valentin wouldn't. Still, I watched Luka while I tried to spot the other man.

Finlay followed my gaze. "That one's trouble," he warned.

"Looks like my kind of trouble," I murmured, just to see what he'd say.

"Only if you like 'em big and dumb."

I grinned at him. "You just described the perfect man."

Finlay threw his head back and laughed. He clapped me on the shoulder. "You got a name, Lady Mystery?"

"Dahlia," I said.

He lifted his glass. "It's always my pleasure to meet a beautiful woman."

We spent half an hour talking about inconsequential things. I kept an eye out for the hooded stranger and didn't find him, but I did occasionally see Luka working his way through the crowd, beer in hand. Finlay told me about the bar—he'd owned it for over fifteen years and had come up with the concept of a bar with a completely dark interior during a night of drinking with friends. They'd told him it wouldn't work and he'd set out to prove them wrong.

He had. In the time that I'd been here, I'd seen one rando wander in without being able to see, and the bouncer had quickly escorted him out of the building. Everyone else, from the bartender to the patrons, had augmented vision or lenses like mine that let them see in the dark. With mercenary clientele, augments weren't unusual and the concept was interesting enough to draw a crowd.

Eventually the conversation worked its way back to me. He looked me over, but his gaze was more professional curiosity than personal interest. "What sort of business are you in?"

"Hunting. Retrieval. Cleaning. I do whatever needs to be done."

"So you were serious earlier? You're going to hunt the rebels."

"Yes." I leaned closer and he bent my way. In a low voice, I said, "But I don't think it's rebels at all. At least not Rogue rebels."

His gaze sharpened, as if he were trying to see under my hat. "What makes you think that?" he asked quietly.

"Intuition."

"Bah," he scoffed with a wave. "You haven't been alive long enough to develop intuition. Come back when you're my age."

I smiled into my second beer. Finlay glanced at me again and a frown creased his forehead when I remained silent.

"Aren't you going to tell me I'm wrong?" he finally asked.

"Would it do any good?"

He chuckled quietly. "Maybe you have intuition after all. Who do you think is behind the attack?"

"I'll tell you, but only if we're working together. I'll do an eighty-twenty split of any bounty the attackers bring in if your information leads me to them."

"Sixty-forty."

"You really *do* think I was born yesterday."

"How do I know you won't just take the money and disappear?"

I stared at him for a long moment, weighing my options. I hadn't seen Luka in a while, and I didn't see him now. I'd rather he not get confirmation of my past, though if he dug deep enough, he'd find the connections anyway.

Finally, I pulled a black, square card from one of my inside coat pockets. A rosette of an eight-pointed dahlia was embossed on the front in glittering gold. On the back was the address of a secure digital dropbox.

Finlay's eyes widened and he snatched the card from my hand before surreptitiously looking around to see if anyone was paying attention. "What are you doing?" he hissed. "Everyone knows the Golden Dahlia retired years ago. If she catches you impersonating her, she'll do more than kill you."

"Semi-retired," I said. When he still looked skeptical, I said, "Check the address. It hasn't changed. Send me a message."

His expression went distant as he accessed the net.

I opened the dropbox. Because the address hadn't changed, I still got messages, I just ignored most of them.

When the message came through, I raised an eyebrow. "I'm not going to pay you ten thousand credits to let me know where the imposter is, but nice try."

He sucked in a breath. "Holy shit." He said it quietly, drawing out the syllables. "Why are you here?"

"Business, as I said. Business that you can help me with."

"I didn't expect you to be so tiny," he said. "Did you really—"

I cut him off. "No one ever does, and yes, probably. Now, do we have an agreement?"

He shook himself. "Fine. Seventy-thirty, but that's as low as I'll go."

"Deal." It was the standard split I'd been aiming for from the beginning. I held out my hand and we shook on it.

There was a new wariness to him now. Finlay hadn't become a successful businessman by being stupid, and my reputation proceeded me. It'd been blown a bit out of proportion, as all rumors were, but there was enough truth in it that he was right to be cautious.

"Who do you think it is?" he asked.

I kept my voice low. The background music and ambient conversation would mask us from all but the most sensitive hearing augments. "I have reason to believe it's Quint, either military or mercenary. Have you heard anything about a new crew in town?"

"New crews turn up constantly in Koan," he said. "Though not too many from the Confederacy. I haven't heard anything specific, but I'll put out some feelers, see what my people can find. Should I use this address?" He patted the pocket where he'd put my card.

"Yes. I believe they're being led by an older man with reddish-brown hair, graying at the temples. He may or may not be going by Adams. And have your people be careful. I don't think this crew much cares about collateral damage."

"My people know how to stay invisible."

That's what I was counting on and why I'd wanted to visit the bars in the first place. His network would be far better than one woman futilely scouring the city. Of course, that information highway worked both ways. In the unlikely event that someone was looking for the Golden Dahlia in Koan, I'd just given Finlay the perfect setup.

I drained the last of my beer. "Thanks for the drink. Keep me posted on what you find."

He shook his head in wonder. "Never thought I'd see the day that you darkened my door, but I'm glad you did. I'll send the word tonight for my people to keep their eyes open. It was a pleasure, Lady Mystery."

I exited the bar and made my way back to our rendezvous point. I took a circuitous route to ensure I wasn't being followed, then added another two blocks when I thought I caught sight of the edge of a long coat. When I looped back, the alley was empty. Twenty minutes later, Luka approached from the opposite direction.

"Is Valentin out tonight?" I asked.

Luka frowned and glanced around, looking for his wayward charge. "He's not supposed to be. Why?"

"I saw someone who seemed familiar, but I couldn't place him. Learn anything?"

"Everyone is talking about the attack. The Rogue rebel rumor is spreading here, too. You and Finlay looked cozy."

"He's going to ask around, see if he hears anything about a crew that doesn't belong."

"Out of the goodness of his heart?" Luka managed to convey his skepticism without altering his tone.

I laughed quietly. "No, because I promised him thirty percent of the bounty. I hope Valentin doesn't mind paying up."

———

WE WENT TO BLACKHEART NEXT. The crowd was rougher, noisier, and looking for trouble. Luka got in a brawl with two young men too stupid to recognize the threat he presented. He laid them out with a single punch each, but then he was quickly tossed out.

I wasn't much more successful. While I didn't *exactly* get in a fistfight, I planted a fair number of elbows in kidneys and other soft tissues. No one I talked to had enough connections to find the team we were searching for. And while everyone was talking about the attack, no one seemed to have any information other than what the news outlets were reporting.

Jack's was moderately better. Luka didn't get thrown out, and he contacted some people who promised to keep an eye out for a cut of the bounty. I talked to Jack, the owner, briefly, but he was more interested in getting in my pants than earning credits. His attention didn't stray above my chest long enough for me to determine if he had an information network or not, so that was a failure.

All of my hopes rested on Finlay because I didn't know how good Luka's contacts actually were.

I'd kept an eye out, but I hadn't spotted the man in the coat again.

The sky was starting to lighten by the time we returned to the palace. We entered through a smaller side tunnel that seemed suspiciously like a secret passageway, albeit one with five locked doors along its length. "Why not use the tunnel we used before?" I asked.

"Palace staff are arriving for the day."

"Ah." It would definitely look bad for a foreign queen to be caught sneaking in with Valentin's closest guard. I needed to sleep before I had lunch with Margie or she'd wrangle every secret from my exhausted brain.

Luka escorted me to the door of my suite. "Do you want me to check your rooms?" he asked.

"No, thank you. And thank you for going with me tonight."

He nodded silently and turned for Valentin's suite. So much for our bonding time.

I let myself into the suite. Imogen stood from the sofa and looked me over.

"Any injuries?"

"No. But you missed Luka in action. Two dumbasses decided he was a good target."

"Is he hurt?" She sounded concerned.

"He might've bruised his knuckles on their faces. Otherwise, no."

She grinned. "Was it beautiful? I sparred with him in the gym. He moves like liquid."

"It was beautiful," I agreed before changing the subject. "We're having lunch with the dowager empress today. Before that, I'd like to go talk to Myra Shah and get her insight on the advisors. I'm going to grab a couple of hours of sleep. Please be ready to leave by ten. You're on your own for breakfast."

"I'll survive, somehow," she said, her voice desert dry. "I'm glad you're back in one piece. Sleep well."

"Thank you."

I was stripping out of my gear when Valentin linked to me. *Luka just got back. Are you okay?*

Valentin was in his suite, as expected, not out on the streets of Koan, unprotected. Relief burned through me, and I realized I'd been worried for him.

Yes, just tired, I replied. *We didn't get anything definite, but we have a couple of leads. Now I'm going to crash for a few hours. Then I'm planning to go see Myra Shah before lunch with your mom. Come find me after lunch?*

Of course. Sleep well. I'm glad you're safe.

Warmth bloomed in a gentle wave. The knife-sharp pain and rage I felt every time I thought about *Invictia* eased, just a bit. When I'd lost my ship, I'd lost a piece of me, but I was still alive to fight, and I had friends who cared. *Valentin* cared. And while I loved our explosive chemistry, I craved that caring just as much. I longed for someone to stand by my side, to know all of me and love me anyway. Deep in my secret heart, I hoped it would be Valentin.

My fury and sorrow were still there, but now they were tempered with patience and care and hope. I would weather this storm as I had all that came before.

And then I would rain hell on whoever was responsible.

12

I'd gotten three and a half hours of sleep. It wasn't enough, and now I stared stupidly at my wardrobe, unable to decide what to wear. I wanted to go see *Invictia* before I ambushed Myra in her office, then I had a lunch scheduled with the dowager empress. I wouldn't have time to change.

Margie had been nice enough last night, but she was also effortlessly elegant in a way I could never hope to match. So should I attempt a poor copy of it by wearing one of my day dresses, as Stella had called them, or just go for comfort with slacks and a blouse?

I'd asked Valentin for advice. His completely useless response had been "be yourself," as if I had lunch with empresses every day. To make matters worse, I didn't know if I was walking into a friendly chat or a polite interrogation.

I couldn't very well poke around *Invictia*'s wreckage in a dress, so that narrowed my choices. Done with indecisiveness, I pulled out a pair of slim charcoal slacks and a deep teal, tunic-length blouse. It limited my weapon options, but taking weapons to lunch with the former empress was probably a faux pas anyway. I put on my ankle boots and checked myself in the mirror. I looked good enough.

I met Imogen in the living room. She had opted for black slacks and a white shirt. A black jacket was draped over the back of the sofa, which would cover her shoulder holster. She was going for a very professional look today.

"Ready?" she asked.

"As ready as I'm going to be."

"Are you worried about Myra or the empress?"

"Why not both?" I asked with a smile.

She grinned. "You'll do fine. They both seemed to like you."

I hoped that held true this morning.

"Are you armed?" Imogen asked.

"I have a short knife tucked in my pocket, but I don't have any guns. Think I should change that?"

"I have two. If it comes down to it, you can have one of them," Imogen said. "Both ladies might take it better if you didn't show up armed."

"Did you think we'd be fighting off an army today or are you always this prepared?"

Imogen smirked. "With you, one never knows."

I laughed at the well-deserved hit. "I'm glad that the biggest drama in Arx right now is who is going to win the cooking competition."

"Heard about that, did you?" Imogen chuckled. "I've got ten credits on Zita. Like taking candy from babies."

We shared a grin.

I linked Valentin as we left the suite. He accepted and immediately asked, *Is everything okay?* It was like he thought I got into trouble on a regular basis or something.

Everything is fine. I just wanted to let you know that I'm heading out to the spaceport, then I'm going to go talk to Myra. She's not expecting me, but I want to get her opinion on a few of the advisors. After that, I have lunch with your mom.

Do you want me to go with you to visit your ship?

I did, desperately, but the spaceport was public and I needed to keep it together. I couldn't let the attackers see just how big of a wound they'd left. And going alone sent its own message, one that could be easily misinterpreted as Valentin withdrawing his support.

Thank you, the offer means a lot to me, but I need to go alone.

You're taking Imogen?

I am, and she's already informed me that she has two guns.

Good. I'm also sending a security team to keep an eye on things. Also, there was a hit on the image recognition algorithm. A woman that looks eerily similar to the sketch of Werner's contact works for the domestic affairs department as a junior analyst.

Isn't that Asmo's department?

It is.

Well, wasn't that interesting. *Are you bringing her in?*

Not yet, he said. *The query isn't finished, so I don't want to tip our hand too early in case there are more matches.*

I understood his caution, but I itched to act now. *Keep me posted.*

Will do. I'm in my private office today. Let me know if you need anything. I'll see you after lunch.

I thanked him and cut the connection. I was very tempted to head to his suite, just to see him as I passed by, but it sounded like he was working. Maybe I would see if I could steal him away for the afternoon once I was done with my obligations.

Or maybe he would like to go with me to pick up a junior analyst who wanted me gone.

We took the elevator down to the ground floor, went through two sets of locked doors, and finally came out in the palace's main atrium. It was open all the way to the distant glass roof and decorated in ornate carved stone and gilded plaster. This was the main entrance to the palace, designed to flaunt the wealth and power of the Kos Empire—and it did.

A dozen people stood looking around in awe, part of a tour group, and a dozen more hurried toward the various hallways leading off the main chamber. A man and a woman in Imperial Guard uniforms casually patrolled the space.

No one stopped us as we headed for the exit closest to the spaceport. Once outside, the path took us through the gardens. Soldiers in Kos uniforms were stationed at regular intervals along the route. I tried to enjoy the lovely scenery, but the closer we got, the tighter my nerves wound.

My first glimpse of *Invictia* punched me in the gut. My beautiful baby was a hollow husk.

I locked down my emotions behind a wall of ice, and my gait did not falter as I neared. I had hoped to salvage what I could, but there was nothing left. Nothing. After the initial explosion, the stardrive had burned too hot. The fire crews were gone, but the ground remained wet, a testimony to how long the drive had burned. Part of the outer hull remained, but the interior was a spiderweb of twisted, melted metal.

It was so much worse in the morning light, even worse than watching it burn.

I visually searched the wreckage for my quarters, but found only a void where they should've been. My armory was gone, as were the few mementos I'd kept through the years and hadn't moved to Arx. The first gun I'd bought myself with money I'd earned on my own. A chair more comfortable than beautiful. A piece of art painted by a street kid as payment for taking care of the men bothering him.

I briefly closed my eyes as each loss stabbed deep. Imogen remained absolutely, thankfully silent.

This attack felt personal. It might've helped the rumors of Rogue rebels, but it felt like a private, vicious *fuck you*. And I knew of exactly one person with the troops, firepower, and desire to send this particular message: Commander Tony Adams.

I'd outsmarted him twice and he wanted payback. He'd gotten it, but I would not give him the satisfaction of seeing me break down. I gazed at the wreckage for a few minutes longer, giving the pain time to morph into anger and resolve, and then turned on my heel and walked away.

"Let's go see Myra," I said. "We have some traitors to find."

———

THE COURTYARD on the other side of the palace was paved with cobblestones that looked like they had been here since the building had first been constructed. A narrow strip of green garden shielded the courtyard from the modern glass tower next door that held most of the government offices and the advisors' apartments.

We entered the tower along with a steady stream of other people. A woman in an Imperial Guard uniform was stationed next to the door. The foyer looked exactly like I would expect in any high-end office building in the system. A gilt-framed portrait of Valentin hung over the reception desk, but everything else was sleek, modern, and a little sterile.

I wondered if Myra had her guards reporting on my movements or if I would surprise her. I'd looked up her office location this morning. If she wasn't there, I'd also looked up the addresses of the Imperial Guard headquarters and her home. Myra Shah was not escaping this conversation.

A pair of curved staircases led up to the second-floor balcony, one on each side of the front desk. We took the stairs on the left. The second floor was rectangular, wider than it was deep, with an elevator bank tucked into an alcove on the back wall. This floor contained six office suites, two on each side of the building. These were the offices of the top-level advisors and their assistants. The rest of the peons were in smaller cubicles on higher floors.

The frosted double doors of the closest office proclaimed it belonged to Hannah Perkins. The next set of doors led to Oskar Krystopa's office. I hurried past and hoped they were both busy with other things.

I pulled open the door to Myra's office suite and found her standing next to her assistant's empty desk. She looked like she was waiting for me, so that answered the question of whether or not she was monitoring my movements.

She was dressed casually in black utility pants and a form-fitting blue knit shirt. Today, she looked more like the guards she advised than an imperial advisor, especially with the plasma pistol strapped around her waist. Imogen tensed beside me, but she didn't interfere.

"You came this far, so you might as well come on back to my office," Myra said. She didn't sound particularly happy to see me, but since she didn't kick me out, I assumed she'd decided to help. We followed her down a short hall to another door, this one solid wood. Imogen stuck to me like glue. I might somewhat trust Myra, but Imogen was taking no chances.

The office was large, with windows lining the left and back walls looking out over the gardens. A delicate wooden desk anchored the middle of the space and two padded chairs faced it. Myra settled behind her desk and waved me to a chair in front of it. I sat and Imogen hovered near the door, far enough away to give us the illusion of privacy.

"I'm sorry about your ship," Myra said. "I already spoke to Advisor Krystopa about the security failure. His team is looking into it."

Pain stabbed at me. I hid it behind a sigh. "In that case, I won't hold my breath on the investigation results."

Myra grimaced. "You are not his favorite person," she confirmed. "But Valentin has ordered a full investigation, so Oskar will do it quickly enough, he'll just bitch about it."

"So you don't think Oskar is a traitor?"

She pinned me with a direct stare. Instead of answering the question, she asked, "Would you like to tell me why you and Luka were out in Koan last night?"

"No."

She hadn't expected that answer and it threw her for a second. "Why not?"

Two could play this game. I answered her question with a question of my own. "How did you know we were out?"

"One of my guards saw you at Jack's. Well, she saw Luka and a petite figure in a coat and hat."

Ah, so she'd been fishing and gotten lucky when I didn't flat out deny it. "Did the guard tell anyone else?"

"No. And I told her to keep it to herself. I believe she will."

"I was looking into the attack."

She leaned forward. "Did you find anything?"

"Not yet."

"Damn." She sighed and rubbed her face. "I don't think Oskar is a traitor, but I don't have any proof one way or another. Same for Junior. But they are both my friends and I'm biased."

"But you *do* think there is a traitor."

She nodded slowly.

I had to be careful here to not let my own biases cloud my

judgement. "Hannah, Joanna, and Asmo seemed very chummy before dinner last night."

"Oskar, Junior, and I are friends, and Hannah, Joanna, and Asmo are friends, or at least friendlier with each other than with the rest of us. Hannah keeps the other two in line. Mostly. Joanna is more likely to break from the group than Asmo when it comes to votes."

"Do you have any feelings on who might be betraying Valentin?"

She tapped her fingers on her desk while she decided if she was going to trust me. After a few seconds, she said, "I have many feelings and exactly zero proof. I've done as much digging as I can without being obvious about it, and they are all super clean. I can't stand Asmo, but on paper, the man is a saint."

"But you think he's dirty?"

"I couldn't say."

She might not have wanted to voice her opinion directly, but her expression made the truth clear enough—she thought Asmo wasn't as clean as he appeared to be.

"Tell me about him. What's his story?" I'd done my own research, but she might know something I didn't.

"Asmo Copley is from a very old, very powerful, very respected family. They run one of the largest shipbuilding companies in the Empire."

I'd known that already, but I played along. "Copley Heavy Industries? That's his family's business?"

"Yes. His older sister is being trained to take over the company while Asmo focuses on politics."

"And as the domestic affairs advisor, I'm sure he's totally impartial about issues that could potentially affect his family."

"I'm sure," Myra murmured. She was being cautious, but I

didn't hold it against her. Having a Copley for an enemy would not be an enviable position. "A year or two ago, there were some quiet rumors that the family was struggling financially, but nothing ever came of it. They continue to spend credits like water."

I perked up. I hadn't found those rumors during my research, which meant the family had spent a lot of time and effort erasing them. And money was a powerful motivator. "Would he work with Quint against the Empire?"

"I couldn't say, but Asmo is an expert at judging which situations are to his advantage, and he is known to use all available resources to achieve his goals."

So, in a word, *yes*.

I asked about the other advisors. Joanna, the science and technology advisor, and Junior, the medical advisor, had both risen rapidly through the diplomatic ranks thanks to intelligence, dedication, and passion for the work. Both tended to keep to themselves more than the other advisors, but they often worked together thanks to their overlapping fields. Joanna had lost a much younger sister in the war a few years ago and had retreated even further into her work in medical technology.

Oskar had been the military strategy advisor for years and thought his word should be law. He was training his daughter to take over for him, and the young woman was smart and well liked, but Oskar showed no signs that he was ready for retirement just yet.

When I asked if any of them would work with Quint, I got flat denials. Other than that, Myra was careful to stick to factual statements, positive opinions, and well substantiated rumors. She trusted me, but only so far.

"And Hannah?" I prompted when it seemed she was going to skip the woman entirely.

"Hannah Perkins has been a diplomat for over fifty years, and she's been the diplomatic relations advisor for nearly thirty. She has the most connections of any of us, in part because of her tenure and in part because she is married to the emperor's cousin. She lost two sons in the war and she hates all things Quint with fanatical passion."

Hate was a powerful motivator, as was power. "Is her husband in line to inherit the throne?"

"No, Leo is Valentin's distant cousin, and that family has many branches. I think he was fifth or sixth in line when Valentin's father died."

I filed that information away. "If she hates Quint, then she wouldn't work with them?"

"No." Myra paused and tapped her fingers, staring into the middle distance. I let my gaze wander while she organized her thoughts. The green garden outside was strangely hypnotic after living in Arx. There, we had a perpetual view of rocks and snow, and while I'd had ceiling panels installed to mimic blue skies, nothing beat the real thing.

"No, she would not help Quint. But she might use them."

It was the most forthright statement she'd made so far. I pressed my luck. "Do you think she is working against Valentin?"

"I couldn't say."

I had pressed her as far as she was willing to go, so I changed the subject. "Do you know of anyone else that would have a reason to betray Valentin? What about his assistant?"

"Lewis?" she asked in surprise. "No, I can't imagine. He's been with Valentin for years. I've never caught any weird vibes from him, and I've worked with him a lot to coordinate Valentin's security. He's a good guy."

So I was back to Asmo and Hannah, maybe. I fought the urge to rub my eyes in frustration. "Do you have any guards that are my size or any spare uniforms that will fit me?"

Myra frowned. "Why?"

"Because Imperial Guards are nearly as invisible as regular staff and people tend to question them less."

Her scowl deepened. "And you know this how?"

I was saved from having to answer by the shrill shriek of the building's fire alarm.

"Not again," Myra muttered.

"Is this common?"

"For the last three days, yes. Maintenance thinks there must be rats in the wiring. But they make us evacuate anyway."

I stood. "You didn't find the timing odd? Is the palace affected?"

I tried to link to Valentin, but he didn't answer. Neither did Luka. Dread settled in my stomach. Something was wrong, I could feel it.

"The systems are connected," Myra said with a frown.

"Can you pull up the surveillance footage from Valentin's floor?"

"Only if it's an emergency."

"It is. I'll take the blame."

Either my tone or the situation must've persuaded her. She tapped on her console, scowled, and tapped some more. "Surveillance is down," she murmured.

That's all I needed to hear. I hit the door at a run, Imogen on my heels.

13

I held out a hand and Imogen passed me one of her pistols. A sizable crowd of people milled about in the lobby despite the ongoing alarm. A few people halfheartedly headed outside as requested by the overwhelmed security guards, but most stood between me and the door. I didn't want to cause a stampede, but if these people didn't get out of my way, I wasn't going to be held responsible.

Myra caught up to us and then shoved ahead, her own pistol visible. "MOVE! Imperial Guard coming through!" Her shouts echoed off the ceiling, and a path magically opened up.

The courtyard was filled with disgruntled people dressed in nice clothes. Luckily, they were spread out enough that we didn't have to elbow our way through. But getting into the palace nearly took an act of violence. We had to fight against the crowd coming out, and then Myra stopped to argue with the security guard who tried to usher us back outside. As soon as the guard was distracted, I bolted for the stairs.

"Stop!" she shouted.

I ignored her. Hopefully Myra would keep her from shooting

me in the back.

The elevators were out of service, but the doors at the bottom of the private stairs to the family wing unlocked with my personal identity key. Valentin had added me to the system.

"Plan?" Imogen asked as we raced up the stairs.

"Shoot anything that shoots at us. Find Valentin. Don't get shot."

"Your planning sucks."

I chuckled. She wasn't wrong. We were both augmented with speed and strength, so six stories of stairs weren't a challenge. I remained on guard, but the stairwell was empty. If this was an attack and not a freaky coincidence, the attackers were either still on the floor or they'd escaped another way.

The electronic lock on the door at the top of the stairs was dead and only the emergency lights were on. I hadn't put in my night-vision lenses this morning, so if it was dark on the other side of this wall, I was going to be fucked.

But first, we had to get through the door. I tried linking to Valentin and Luka again, but they still didn't answer. Panic pushed my pulse faster, but the door was locked tight. "Think we can kick it down?"

Imogen looked skeptical but shrugged gamely. "On three?"

We slammed our feet into the door near the lock. It made a hellacious noise, but it held firm. After four attempts with the same result, I began to wonder if I was going to have to climb the elevator shaft. I could do it, but it would take time, and Valentin still hadn't answered any of my attempts to link with him.

I heard a faint *thunk*, then the door unlocked and swung open an inch. I dove for the handle while Imogen covered the opening.

"Luka?" she asked.

I peeked around the door. It took me a second to recognize the big guard. He slumped against the doorframe, blood painting his blond hair red. The hallway beyond him was dim, a distant window providing the only light. Even the emergency lights were off.

"Where is Valentin?" I demanded.

"He's here. Got a trauma-doc on him. He needs medical." Luka's voice was thick and sluggish.

"Threats?" Imogen asked.

"Team of five. Two are down in the hall, likely dead. Three more ran after they downed Valentin. Wearing guard uniforms. I hit at least two of them."

Imogen moved into the hall, scanning for threats. I locked down the desire to rush in headlong to find Valentin and cautiously followed her. I glanced down at Luka. "Is anyone else injured? Are you stable?"

"No and I'll survive," he said.

Valentin lay a meter down the hall with a trauma-doc clamped around his chest. Even in the low light, I could see that he was deathly pale. From the blood trail, it seemed like Luka had carried Valentin from the direction of his office, then collapsed. Luka had dragged himself to the door, leaving Valentin tucked into a shallow nook. Farther down the hall, two bodies were partially hidden by the faint light. They weren't moving.

I smothered my fear and anger and dealt with the most important issues first. "Where was Valentin hit?"

"Plasma bolt to the chest, right side."

"Do you trust the medical team here?" I asked.

"I trust Junior," he said.

If he said anything after that, I didn't hear it. Valentin was pale, still, and blood-soaked. For a brief, terrifying second, I thought he was already dead. I froze out of sheer instinct, my heart racing, before I pushed myself through it. Some people fell apart in dangerous situations, and I didn't blame them. Instinct and self-preservation were incredibly powerful. But I had training and experience to fall back on, so I pushed aside everything except ruthless determination.

I bent, pressed my fingers to Valentin's neck, and nearly passed out from relief when I detected a faint, thready pulse. It was still a bad sign, but I had a chance to keep him alive if I could get him to medical fast enough.

I picked him up as carefully as I could. He didn't stir when I lifted him. The edge of the trauma-doc pressed into my chest, and I tried my very best not to think of him as dead weight. Chest wounds were dangerous and often fatal, even with help from advanced technology. I suppressed the fluttery panic that tried to rise. I had to get him to medical *now*. I turned for the stairs, then remembered Luka was waiting on me.

"Link Junior and tell him to meet me in medical."

"Can't," Luka said. "Whatever took out the lights took out my neural link."

Fuck. "Where is medical?"

"On the second floor."

"Can you carry him?" I asked Imogen, tilting my head at Luka. She nodded, so I stepped around her into the stairwell.

"Where are you hit? Can I put you over my shoulders?" she asked him.

"Left side, left thigh, right calf, right arm. Do what you have to do."

Footsteps in the stairwell preceded Myra. She skidded to a stop when she caught sight of me. Several guards hovered behind her. She took in the scene in a glance. "Is he alive?" she asked.

"Barely. Luka can't link. Ask Junior to meet us in medical, now. Two down in the hall, possibly still alive. Find the three who escaped. Luka said they're in guard uniforms and two of them are injured."

124

She turned to the guards behind her. "Secure the floor. Search the premises. No one in or out without my express permission, guards included."

They saluted and edged around us, sneaking glances at Valentin's still form. Imogen heaved Luka up and draped his large form over her shoulders. His face was a mask of pain but he didn't make a single sound.

"Let's go," I said.

Myra led us down the stairs at a quick trot. I was strong enough to carry Valentin cradled like this, but my back and arm muscles burned as I tried my best to keep him from jostling on each step.

An eternity later, we arrived on the second floor and made the short trip to medical, where Junior was waiting for us. When he saw Valentin's state, deep lines bracketed his mouth.

"Plasma pulse through the chest, right side," I said. "Luka got him in the trauma-doc an unknown amount of time after the hit."

"Less than two minutes," Luka grated out.

"He's been unresponsive since before I picked him up."

"Put him here, carefully," Junior said with a wave to the nearest med chamber. The chamber was just long and wide enough for a single person, with a clear hood that sealed over the flat surface for the patient. It was the newest model, far superior to anything we had in Arx. A small army of doctors and nurses moved around the room, gathering supplies and programming the auto-doc.

I set Valentin down and the machine started beeping. They were not happy beeps. Junior took over, tapping the control panel with quick, precise movements.

I watched, helpless. Myra hovered at my shoulder. Behind us, Luka argued with another doctor. He refused to be put under while Valentin was defenseless. Unfortunately for him, his slurred voice meant he wasn't going to be awake for much longer anyway.

This was one problem I could solve. I turned to Luka. "The sooner you heal, the sooner you can protect Valentin, so shut up, lie down, and let the doctors do their jobs. I will guard him while you're out."

Luka glared. "You're the reason he's injured. If he hadn't been so distracted by you, he wouldn't have been ambushed in his own fucking office."

The verbal dagger hit true. Valentin *had* survived multiple attempts on his life with barely a scratch. But then I'd shown up and he'd been attacked twice in two days. Now he teetered on the edge of death.

I walled off my emotions and stared down at Luka with cool dispassion. "Do not blame me for your own failures. Get in the fucking med chamber so next time you might actually be able to do your fucking job."

Luka tried to lunge for me, but Imogen easily pinned him down on the med chamber table. His pallor was emphasized against her deep brown skin. He'd lost a lot of blood. Despite my harsh words, I was impressed he'd made it as far as he had.

"Sedate him," Junior ordered behind me.

Luka growled something, but the doctor nearest him pressed an injector to his arm while Imogen held him still. He glared at me until his eyes slipped closed. This would not improve our relationship.

I glanced around. There were too many people in here. Valentin was in the med chamber, fitted with a full-face breathing mask. That was a bad sign. It meant that they planned to fill the chamber with renewal fluids to supplement the work of the auto-doc.

They'd cut away most of his clothes. His golden skin had lost its luster. He, too, had lost a lot of blood. What the fuck had happened?

"Okay, on three, we're removing the trauma-doc. Tanya, I want you standing by to flood the chamber as soon as we're clear."

"Yes, Dr. Mobb," a petite red-haired woman said.

Junior removed the trauma-doc with the help of two nurses. The med chamber shrieked a warning as Valentin's vitals plummeted. I held my breath as they quickly and carefully arranged Valentin in the middle of the operating table, then closed the chamber lid. Tanya tapped on the control screen and a thick, pinkish fluid poured over Valentin's body.

Junior took over the controls. "Come on, come on," he murmured like a prayer.

I watched over his shoulder as he tweaked setting after setting, and I found myself echoing his words, my heart in my throat, helpless to do anything but watch as the chamber continued to wail. The hole in Valentin's chest was a mass of cauterization and renewal gel from the trauma-doc.

I wished Stella was here, with her gift for healing and her no-nonsense bedside manner.

After what felt like an age, Valentin's vitals stabilized. They remained dangerously low, but they weren't worsening, so that was a tiny bit of good news. My eyes felt gritty and my chest hurt. I didn't dare feel relief, yet, though. I didn't want to give the universe a reason to snatch him away.

"Do you need all of these people?" I asked Junior quietly.

Myra, still hovering near, said, "Keep the ones you trust most and send the rest home. I've got guards on the way to protect the hallway, but I'm putting this room on lockdown."

Junior frowned at us. "You think he's in danger from my people?"

"Someone wants him dead. It's my job to keep him alive," Myra said. "Send them home. Make sure whoever you keep knows we'll be locked in until he wakes."

Junior sent a significant glance my way. "I hope you know what you're doing," he said to Myra. She nodded at him, and he capitulated. Junior kept four people and sent the rest home.

After they left, Myra turned to me. "In or out? Once I lock this door, I'm not opening it until Valentin is awake."

I would be more useful if I weren't trapped inside, but I couldn't bring myself to leave Valentin when he was so vulnerable and Luka was out of commission. "In."

She nodded and manually locked the door with a lock that was only accessible from the inside. The quiet beeping of the med chambers was loud in the silence. Only the two chambers containing Luka and Valentin were filled.

"Where are the captured soldiers?"

Junior looked up from Valentin's med chamber controls and shook his head. "One died late last night and the other passed early this morning." When he caught my suspicious glance, his jaw firmed and his eyes flashed. "They weren't killed, if that's what you're thinking. I'm surprised they survived as long as they did. Neither regained consciousness and I had to manually program the auto-doc because it originally put their chance of survival too low to initiate treatment. I was here for both deaths and did everything I could."

"I apologize. It's been a shitty twenty-four hours." I swore. "Has anyone talked to Margie?"

Myra's expression went distant. "The empress's bodyguard Rina says Marguerite is in her private garden and unharmed. I've advised them to seek protective shelter immediately."

"Were the other attackers caught?"

Myra's pinched look was answer enough.

An hour later, Junior sighed and stopped his constant fiddling with the med chamber controls. The beeps sounded less ominous than they had when Valentin had first gone in. He turned to me and Myra. "The worst is past. He'll pull through. He has healing augments, and the med chamber will do the rest."

I wasn't sure if he was reassuring us or himself.

———

MEDICAL HAD BEEN DESIGNED as a refuge. It was stocked with water, rations, and a small bunk room, but the monotony of waiting left far too much time for thinking. The nurses had set up a rotation schedule and then two of them had disappeared into the bunks despite the fact that it had been morning. I supposed they were used to odd shifts.

Junior checked on Valentin every ten minutes like clockwork. Myra situated herself in a corner where she could see everyone, but her distant expression meant she was linking. I sat next to Valentin's med chamber and Imogen leaned against the wall nearby. I sent a message to Ari, letting her know that I was okay.

Despite his augmented healing, Valentin remained unconscious. His vitals had stabilized, but Junior warned that he would likely remain out for at least a day and would need to remain where he was for several days after that. Tonight's formal dinner had been canceled with the excuse that Valentin had taken ill.

After Margie's guard had gotten her to safety, the dowager empress linked me and demanded details. I had to tell her that Valentin was gravely injured and that we wouldn't open the door, even for her. She took the news only marginally better than the advisors we'd locked out.

Oskar, Hannah, and Asmo had all demanded entry and vowed to arrest us for treason when Myra had refused. Rumors were rampant that Rogue rebels had infiltrated the palace, and with Valentin out of commission, they grew unchecked.

Time crawled. We'd been stuck in here for less than four

hours, but already the inaction made me want to climb the walls. As my worry lessened, my anger grew. Someone had let attackers into the palace to kill Valentin.

They had been very nearly successful.

I'd already lost a ship; I refused to lose Valentin, too. The game had changed and I refused to play by polite rules any longer. I would find the fuckers responsible, even if I had to personally interrogate every one of Valentin's advisors to see it done.

I approached Myra. I still wasn't completely confident she was clean, but I needed backup with clout and she was the best I had. "Have you found any surveillance video?"

Her mouth compressed into an angry line. "Not yet, but I'm working on it."

"If you had to pick three advisors to investigate, who would you pick?" She hesitated, and I slashed a hand through the air. "The time for political bullshit is over. Valentin almost died. I am going to find out who is responsible with or without your help, but it'll go faster if I have an ally."

"Oskar, Asmo, and Hannah."

"You said you didn't think Oskar was a traitor."

"I don't, but I might be wrong, and he has the connections."

I appreciated her frank honesty. "Find me that surveillance video." When she nodded, I retreated back to my place by Valentin.

It was time to dig into financials. I'd worked with a couple of information specialists in the past, so I carefully put together a request. I asked them to focus on Asmo, Oskar, Myra, Lewis, and Hannah. I included a limited search request for Junior and Joanna, just to ensure nothing obvious came up. And I figured I had nothing to lose at this point, so I also asked them to locate Nikolas. If anyone could find him, it would be one of them, and I might as well cover all the bases.

Request sent, I settled in to wait.

It took nine hours for the med chamber to release Luka, which meant he'd been far more injured than he'd let on. He scowled to find me next to Valentin, but after he verified that I hadn't killed the emperor in his sleep, Luka gave me a grudging nod and settled down on the other side of Valentin's med chamber.

I took that for the temporary truce that it was.

Near midnight, Myra and Luka had a low conversation, then Myra headed for the bunks. Luka remained at his post by Valentin. I hoped they had worked out a guarding schedule and Luka wasn't trying to do it all himself.

Imogen found a blanket and made herself a pallet on the floor with her back to the wall. I dozed in my chair near Valentin's med chamber. It wasn't the most comfortable, but it meant I awoke anytime someone came near.

I drifted in the drowsy haze between awake and asleep, so when I heard Valentin's voice in my head, I thought I was dreaming. When it repeated, I startled fully awake and checked on Valentin, but he remained out cold.

It was early, before six, and only Luka remained awake. At his raised eyebrow, I shook my head and settled back into my chair.

When I received a neural link connection from Valentin, I froze for a second before accepting it. *Valentin?*

Yes. Did you forget my identity already? I could hear the mental smile, but he sounded tired and distant.

What happened? Are you okay?

I feel like shit, and I'm barely conscious, but I'm alive, despite the rumors indicating otherwise. But you need to get out of Koan. It's not safe. I've given you access to my ship; it's in the palace spaceport. Take Imogen and go.

I checked the net. The rumors had worsened overnight. Now I stood accused of killing Valentin because he wouldn't help me defeat the Rogue rebels. I was also accused of holding Myra and Junior hostage and forcing them to cover up the emperor's death. There was no mention at all of the attackers who were killed in the family wing. People were pushing for Nikolas to be named emperor and for the Rogue Coalition to be held accountable—seemingly by blowing us out of existence.

I'm not leaving Koan. If you issue a statement and people know you're alive, things will settle down.

There was a long pause. *Maybe. I don't know. The soldiers entered using Nikolas's access codes. I don't know if he was with them, working with them remotely, or tortured into giving up the codes. I didn't sense him nearby, but I only caught a snippet of their communication before they nuked my ability to link.* His tone was completely neutral, but hard proof that his own brother was involved in an attempt on his life had to hurt.

I wished I could touch him, give him a hug. *I'm so sorry.*

I had hoped that he wasn't involved for Mom's sake, but it is not a huge surprise. He sounded resigned. *I've removed his entrance authorization.*

Revoking Nikolas's access was long overdue, but I kept that opinion to myself. Sharing it wouldn't help, even if it was the truth. Margie was going to be crushed—unless she, too, supported Nikolas. But her worry for Valentin had seemed too real and too raw to be an act, so I was inclined to give her the benefit of the doubt until I could talk to her.

Do you think Nikolas is working with Adams? I asked.

I have to assume so until I find evidence otherwise. But without the surveillance video, I have no proof either way.

Proof was the one thing we were short on everywhere.

14

An hour after Valentin drifted back to sleep and left me with more questions than answers, I received a message from Finlay, the owner of Blind and my newest information source. It was flagged urgent and he claimed to have a lead on Adams. Two soldiers with plasma wounds had been brought to a back-alley doctor yesterday afternoon. That wasn't so unusual in itself, but no one had seen them before, they spoke with Quint accents, and they were cagey.

That still wouldn't have been too strange, but when news of the attack hit the wire, Finlay had put two and two together, and had them followed when the doctor released them early this morning. A grainy picture was included that had been cropped to only show a single headshot. Commander Tony Adams wasn't looking directly at the camera but there was no mistaking his identity.

I transferred a small mountain of credits to Finlay's identity and told him the other half was coming when his information proved reliable. I asked for any other information he could give me about the squad, location, and surrounding area.

His response came back far faster than I anticipated. Either he had been waiting for my message or he was super eager to lead me into a trap. He said it looked like the crew was lying low with people rarely leaving the building.

His informant had gotten a peek inside and counted five people, but Finlay warned there could be more. He'd told his man to stay put in a good vantage point and promised updates if the team moved. If this wasn't a trap then Finlay had more than earned all of the promised credits.

I approached Imogen first because I knew she was going to be the hardest to persuade. She wasn't happy until we'd talked through every detail, every alternative, and every fallback. Even then I wouldn't call her happy—more like begrudgingly resigned.

I talked to Myra next because I needed backup to go up against a squad of soldiers, even if Luka had whittled their numbers. I would've preferred my own people at my back, but I didn't have time to wait for them arrive. A loyal, cohesive squad of either Imperial Guards or Kos soldiers would be more trustworthy than an unknown unit of mercenaries hired at the eleventh hour.

Myra wasn't enthusiastic about committing her people, but when she realized I was leading the charge from the front, she reluctantly agreed. She promised me a squad of nine, but warned that she would give their commander autonomy to ignore my orders if it seemed like I was going to get them killed. It wasn't ideal, but I was willing to work with what I had.

By the time Valentin awoke for the second time, my plan was set. No one was entirely happy, but we all agreed that it was the best we could do, given the current information. Without knowing exactly who wanted Valentin dead and who they had in their pocket, we had to limit the information to the fewest number of people possible.

This time, Valentin was awake enough to talk using the microphone built into his face mask. Junior, Myra, and Luka all crowded around the med chamber, peppering him with questions.

"Why haven't you gotten in front of the rumors of Queen Rani's treachery and my death?" he demanded, his voice hoarse.

"We've tried," Myra said into the resulting silence. "No one believed us, not when much juicier gossip was spreading like wildfire."

"Let me out of here so I can make a statement."

"Absolutely not," Junior said. "You haven't healed enough. You'll reopen the wound and injure yourself even more. Your shoulder blade was shattered. Bone takes time to mend."

"You could do a spoken announcement," Myra said. "It won't be as powerful, but I'm with Junior—you can't leave the med chamber yet. You nearly died."

"Save your statement for after I leave medical," I said. "It will be more powerful if I'm not in here influencing you, or pretending to be you, or whatever else the rumors say I'm doing."

"You should've already left Koan," Valentin said. "It's not safe for you here, and I can't protect you while I'm trapped in this damned thing."

There were lots of ears listening, so I said, "*You're* not safe when I'm here. I can disappear into the city until the heat dies down and everyone else can work on killing the rumors and proving you're alive and well."

I linked Valentin while the others argued over what I should do. When he accepted, I said, *I know where Adams is.* I'd debated keeping the secret, but I couldn't ask him to be more open with information and not do the same.

Do not go after him alone. Please wait until I can go with you.

I'm taking Imogen and a squad of Myra's finest. With the rumors spreading, I'm afraid he's either going to leave or plan another attack. Time is of the essence.

Tell me where he is and I'll send two platoons.

Will they get there before someone leaks the information and he moves?

Valentin remained stubbornly silent. I knew he was trying to find a reason to prevent me from being the one to go, but we both knew I was the best person for this particular job.

Wear combat armor. I know Sakimoto didn't win any points with her stunt before, but I believe she is loyal. She can get you the armor and go with you. Her squad is one of the best trained in all of Koan.

I disliked combat armor, but even I could see the advantage of blending in with the other soldiers and being able to move about while invisible. *Do you think her squad is loyal? And can you ask her to come without letting Oskar know?*

He hesitated a beat too long. *It might be best if they don't know who you are. I will arrange it—without Oskar's input. I know you can take care of yourself, but please, please, please be careful.*

I will be. You focus on healing so you can get out of there when I return with Adams's head.

———

WHEN IMOGEN and I casually strolled out of medical, we caught the guards by surprise. Luka slammed the door behind us and locked it, so retreat was not an option. I smiled and tossed a wave at the guards' incredulous faces, then turned and sprinted for the hidden exit. Valentin had made me memorize the route and he had locked down access to just us, so if we could make it to the first door, we'd be in the clear.

He should've been in the middle of ordering the guards to stand down and then making his public statement, but I didn't wait to see if it would take. We slammed into the exit tunnel and the door locked behind us. We exited the palace and disappeared into Koan, taking a convoluted route to our rendezvous point with Sergeant Major Natalie Sakimoto.

I mourned the supplies I'd had to leave behind in my suite, but I'd given Myra and Valentin a detailed list to give to Natalie. She would either show up with what I'd asked for or with a squad of Commander Adams's soldiers. I hoped for the former and planned for the latter. We only had Imogen's two guns between us, but we'd make it work.

We should've been well ahead of Natalie, but we circled the building where we were meeting her twice before entering. The storehouse was big and deserted. Inside, crates were stacked high, but the front quarter of the building had a decent amount of clear space where we could gear up.

Imogen climbed the nearest aisle and found a good place to cover me. I moved so I had protection at my back and was hidden from the door. We settled down to wait.

Noon came and went, and still, Natalie did not arrive. Valentin and I had agreed to limit communication to emergencies and this didn't qualify—*yet*. I checked the news. Rumors were still flying fast and furious, but now people were speculating about where I had gone, if I had somehow brainwashed the emperor, and if I was planning to try to take the Kos Empire for myself.

It would be funny if it wasn't so serious.

A little after one, someone tapped on the door in the agreed upon sequence. That just meant I wouldn't shoot *first*. The door opened and Natalie Sakimoto came through, pushing a cargo sled. The door closed immediately behind her, but that didn't mean a couple of troopers in armor hadn't snuck through with her. I wished I had thermal imaging equipment.

"Samara?" she called.

"Are you alone?"

She immediately turned my way despite the bad acoustics in

here. She had some sort of hearing augment. "I'm alone. Sorry I'm late. The palace is in chaos and it was difficult to get some of the things on your list. Some were impossible. I brought what I could."

"Did anyone follow you?"

"No."

I eased out of cover. No one took a pot shot at me, so maybe my day was looking up. "What did you get?"

"I brought you a combat rifle and an electroshock pistol, but I couldn't get a sniper rifle without a lot of explanation. Also, I brought combat armor for you and your bodyguard. I brought breaching charges and stun grenades, but no explosive grenades. My squad is going to meet us here in an hour for what they think is a training exercise. Are there really Quint soldiers in Koan? They're not Rogue rebels?"

"Kos could wipe the Rogue Coalition out of existence without breaking a sweat. Rogue rebels attacking the emperor makes zero sense. But I have to admit, Quint pinning it on us was a stroke of genius. Rumors don't need to make sense to grab attention if enough people start repeating them."

"Where is your bodyguard?"

"She's watching to ensure you don't try to kill me."

Natalie glanced around at the tall stacks of crates. "That's smart."

"I try," I said drily. "Once I'm suited up, I'll bring her out."

There was no elegant way to get into the stretchy base layer that went under the combat armor, so I didn't even try. I shimmied and hopped my way into it while Natalie did the same with hers. Once I had the armor on and a combat rifle in hand, I called Imogen down. She climbed down from her perch while I kept an eye on our surroundings.

Once we were all in armor, Natalie reviewed the features,

including, most importantly, how to activate the active camouflage that would render us invisible. She had shown us before we
went to the folly, but repetition made it more likely that we would
remember under duress.

"Can you shut down net connections while soldiers are in the
suits?" I asked.

"No, but I can monitor when connections are being made.
Why?"

"Someone is betraying Valentin and they have many eyes and
ears. I want to know if anyone connects out."

"You think one of my soldiers is a traitor?" There was a
dangerous edge to her voice.

"No, I don't, or we wouldn't be having this conversation. But I
want everyone on lockdown, and if someone starts making
connections, I want to know."

She nodded once.

"When Adams attacked Arx, his soldiers were in Kos combat
armor. None of the surveillance I've seen so far indicates that they
brought it with them, but you should know that it's a possibility."

Natalie cursed under her breath. "I will ensure that our armor
only shows our squad as friendlies. There shouldn't be any other
legitimate Kos soldiers in the building, so we'll have to take the
risk."

We went over the plan three times before she was happy with
it. Either Valentin or Myra had gotten the building's blueprint,
and we discussed the various points of entry. She didn't love
breaking into an unknown building, but time wasn't on our side.

I had considered trying to lure Adams to me, but there were
too many unknowns. A straightforward surprise attack would
be our best bet. I hoped to catch Adams in an afternoon lull.
Finlay had kept me posted, and no one had left the building.
They were hunkered down, either because everyone was looking

for the supposed rebels, or because they were planning something new.

Or they were waiting for me to show up so they could murder me. I supposed we would find out soon enough.

When Natalie's team arrived, she told them to disconnect from the net before she explained the mission. Her squad had been with her a long time and didn't bat an eye at the somewhat unusual request. They shot my closed visor a few glances, but no one asked about me or Imogen.

Natalie broke her squad into four two-person teams. We would hit the building from all four sides. It meant we had to be careful about the field of fire, but it gave Adams's squad less opportunity to escape. Our goal was to capture rather than kill whenever possible.

Plan set, the squad closed their visors. My visor's built-in display outlined everyone in the squad in faint green. Thanks to the transponders, the armor recognized our squad members. In addition to the green, Natalie also had gold around her form because she was the commander.

Imogen was outlined in green and purple, indicating a noncombat specialist. I couldn't see my own color, but I should've also been outlined in green and purple. Natalie had explained that the purple was to help the squad keep track of us separately from the rest of the team. That way they would know to protect us and wouldn't be trying to send us hand signals we didn't understand.

Everyone else—including other Kos soldiers—would lack an outline.

Natalie gave the order to activate our camouflage. One by one, soldiers disappeared, but the faint outlines remained, hanging in seemingly empty air. When we activated thermal imaging, the empty air was replaced by red blobs of body heat from the invisible soldiers, outlined in green, gold, and purple. Now we could see enemy soldiers even if they had the same active camouflage tech.

We took a nondescript transport that dropped us off around the corner from the target building. The three teams hitting the far sides of the building left to get into position. One team stayed with us, bringing our total to five. We were going to hit the largest entrance. I was stacked next to last in line despite my protests.

Natalie counted down, and then I heard the breaching charges echo from the other doors before our own door blew open. If my information was bad, I'd just committed ten people to death.

The building was set up like a typical mercenary headquarters: office in front, bunks in the middle, and an open area in the back for storage and gearing up. Adams had been in the open area with crates of gear in the expanded photo Finlay had sent me.

My team hit the door that opened directly to the storage area. The space was large with a high ceiling and smooth plascrete floors. Windows high on the walls let in plenty of light. Towers of dusty crates made for poor visibility, but also gave us a little bit of cover.

Natalie led with quick steps. I scanned the tops of the crates while the soldiers in front of me swept the ground level. When a red blob appeared high on our left—sans green outline that marked them as a friendly—I shot instinctively. The electroshock pistol shorted out the combat armor's camouflage, and an enemy soldier popped into view.

Unfortunately, it also stunned the soldier *inside* the armor and they toppled off the crate. "Heads up!"

The warning was unnecessary because the soldiers in front of me had already turned and followed my shots to their target. They moved aside, and the falling soldier hit the ground with a sickening *splat*. There was no time for regret.

"Son of a bitch," Natalie growled. "They're in our combat

armor. I repeat, enemy combatants are confirmed in Kos combat armor. Mind the transponder signals."

We kept moving.

One of the other teams stunned two soldiers in the bunks and had them restrained. I was working on the assumption that we were dealing with around a dozen soldiers, plus Commander Adams. More than that and secrecy became questionable. Fewer and he wouldn't have been able to attack as often as he had. Four had died in the previous attacks, and now three more were down. Five could be left, which wasn't an insignificant number in close quarters like this.

We came to the end of the line of crates we'd been following. Natalie poked her head around the corner and pulled back with a curse as a plasma pulse slammed into the crate next to her. "Four invisible protecting one visible with an apparent hostage." She turned to me. "Why wasn't I warned this was a potential hostage situation?"

"I didn't know." But I had a bad feeling about who the potential hostage might be.

"Come out and drop your weapons or I'll blow his head off!" Commander Adams demanded.

"And give up your only bargaining chip? I doubt it," I called back before Natalie could respond.

I moved up next to her and peeked around the corner. Sure enough, Adams stood in a circle of camouflaged soldiers. He wore combat armor but had the visor open. He moved slightly and I got a good look at his hostage. My breath caught. The man in his grip looked strikingly like Valentin. Same dark hair, same good looks, but this man lacked Valentin's musculature. *Nikolas.*

Nikolas looked scared. Was he actually being held as a hostage, or was he working with Adams, and this was their fallback escape plan? I couldn't tell, which meant I didn't know if Adams was serious about his threat to kill him. It didn't really matter because none of the other Kos soldiers knew that Nikolas had potentially betrayed Valentin, so I would have to negotiate for Nikolas's release or be branded a traitor myself.

"Ah, the Scoundrel Queen," Adams greeted. He must've recognized my voice. "We meet again. I should've known you'd be here. Have you come to kill Valentin's heir?"

I wouldn't mind getting my hands on Nikolas, but for an inquisition, not a murder. Not unless he'd betrayed his brother, but even then, I'd let the courts sort it out, or I would destabilize Valentin's throne.

I peeked again. I could hit the two front soldiers before they got shots off, but I couldn't hit all four *and* Adams. And Adams was no fool—there wasn't a clear shot at him without taking out his guard.

"Help me!" Nikolas shouted. Adams shook him into silence.

"Adams, you're surrounded. How do you think this is going to go?"

"You're going to let me leave and I'm not going to bring the building down on our heads. When we're good and far away, I'll let this one go."

Natalie swore under her breath again. "Marlow, Guerra, find the explosives," she murmured. "Stay out of sight."

"No can do, I'm afraid," I replied to Adams. "Surrender and tell us who you're working with and I'll plead for clemency for you."

His laugh was not nice. "I've seen your brand of clemency. I think I'll pass." He raised his voice so that all of the Kos soldiers could hear him. "I have the emperor's brother and heir, Nikolas Kos. If anyone moves, he'll be the first to die. The Quint Confederacy will offer asylum and pay a million credits to whoever brings me Samara Rani's corpse right now."

15

Imogen put herself between me and the rest of the Kos soldiers. With the way the past few days had gone, it wasn't a bad call. I tensed and waited to see if anyone would take the bait.

"You better hope you can spend those credits in the afterlife because that's where I'll put you if you try it," Natalie said quietly. "Queen Rani is an ally of Emperor Kos."

"Unless she killed him," a female voice muttered. I only heard it through the helmet speakers, so it must be someone on another team.

"Congratulations, squad. You have Lee to thank for your extra physical training this month."

The other soldiers groaned. "Dammit, Lee, when will you learn to keep your mouth shut?" another woman grumbled. "Maybe we should give *you* to this Quint asshole."

"Enough," Natalie said. "What is the status of the explosives?"

"The building is rigged to blow," a male voice responded. "He's not bluffing. We haven't found the control yet."

"I will also accept a trade of the queen for Nikolas," Adams announced.

"Don't do it," Imogen said.

I rolled my eyes. I might've risked myself on occasion, but only when the odds were in my favor. Taking this bet would be stupid in the extreme, especially because I wasn't convinced that Nikolas actually *was* a hostage and not just a convenient escape plan.

"Any Quint soldier that helps subdue Adams will receive clemency from the emperor," I called. "Adams doesn't care about you. He's going to blow you all up."

"My soldiers aren't cowardly traitors," Adams taunted.

I bit my tongue against the retort I wanted to make about Nikolas. I didn't need to air the emperor's dirty laundry in front of his people.

"I need those explosives gone," I told Natalie quietly. "It's possible the stun rounds will disable the trigger, but it's not a sure thing. You should pull your people back."

"You can't put Nikolas at risk," Natalie said. "He's the heir to the Kos Empire."

"He might *be* the emperor," Lee mumbled just loud enough for the transmitter to pick up. Clearly she hadn't believed that Valentin's public statement from the med chamber was real. I prayed he would have a quick recovery, so he could be seen in public, or my time in Koan was going to be very short.

"Why don't you tell me who's been feeding you information?" I called to Adams. "So I know whom to target next."

"Stop stalling. We're going to leave and you're going to let us, or Nikolas Kos dies. Or maybe that's what you want? Trying to take out Valentin's competition?"

"Don't let that crazy foreign bitch get me killed!" Nikolas shouted.

That didn't exactly sound like someone who would welcome rescue in any form. He'd nearly convinced me that he truly was a hostage, but now I began to doubt it again. Valentin was a hell of an actor; why wouldn't his brother be as well?

"Adams will blow the building as soon as he's clear. We'll have a very narrow window of opportunity," I said. "You need to get your soldiers out to provide cover."

Gunfire echoed through the speakers and a soldier screamed. "There are two guarding the upper level. One of them shot Marlow. I need backup."

More gunfire and cursing followed.

"They're on the move!" another voice shouted.

A peek around the corner showed me two disappearing red blobs and no sign of Adams. Fuck.

"Everybody out now!" Natalie ordered.

I hesitated for a heartbeat, then dashed after Adams. Imogen swore and followed. Two soldiers were waiting for us around the first corner. I hit the first and Imogen hit the second. One of them got a shot off, but it went wide. The delay cost us precious seconds, though, and I could no longer see the other soldiers we were chasing.

The next soldier's green outline was the only thing that saved them from getting a stun round in the face. "Which way?" I demanded. "And where's your partner?"

They didn't respond, but the muzzle of their combat rifle snapped up. Time slowed. I had nonlethal rounds and that made the decision easy. I fired a split second before they did, except they were using lethal rounds. Imogen, already in motion, took the plasma pulse in her shoulder. She crashed into the wall. The other soldier dropped, stunned.

"Pierced my armor and got my shoulder," Imogen gritted out. I scooped her up into a fireman's carry and after a second's hesitation, grabbed one of the still twitching legs of the soldier who'd shot at me. Twenty credits said I'd just found Lee, but I'd drag her sorry ass out anyway, if only to figure out if she was working for Adams from the start or if the offered money had won her over.

"Imogen is down, and one of ours attacked us," I said over the radio. "I've got both, but someone needs to get on Adams now!"

Footsteps pounded around the corner behind me. I turned, too slow. Natalie dashed up to us, her invisible form outlined in green and gold. "Lee!" she shouted. "Where the fuck is Daniels? His transponder is off." She shook Lee's unresponsive form, then stood. "Out now! I've got her."

The door was in sight when Adams proved that—in this case, at least—he was a man of his word. He detonated the explosives. The explosion flashed bright and tossed me to the ground. The armor protected me from the worst of it, but my head rang and afterimage stars blinded me.

Fire, smoke, and debris obscured everything. The thermal imaging built into the visor turned my vision red. The door had been in front of me, but now I was sideways on the ground. Disorientation threatened to send me deeper into the brightly burning building.

"Samara, are you okay?" Imogen asked. I was half on top of her and hadn't moved.

"I'm alive," I said. "You?"

"Same."

Hands pulled me to my feet and helped me pick up Imogen. "The door is straight ahead, five meters," Natalie said. "Adams didn't have enough explosives to bring the building down all at once, but it's weakened and the fire will finish the job. Move, now. And watch your back. I have to help Guerra."

I eased out of the door, gun first, but I needn't have bothered with caution. Adams was long gone.

———

NATALIE HAD LOST two soldiers in the explosion. Daniels had been found outside the building with a plasma wound, a dead Quint soldier, and supposedly no memory of how either had happened. I'd thought he and Lee had been working with Adams, but the holes in his story made me believe he was actually working for *Nikolas*—or for someone who wanted Nikolas on the throne.

Lee had sworn that her armor had malfunctioned. She'd thought we were enemy soldiers and that had been the only reason she'd shot at us. Of course, she'd heard my voice before she'd pulled the trigger, and neither Natalie nor Myra was born yesterday. Both Lee and Daniels were in the brig, awaiting a tribunal hearing.

I'd questioned them yesterday afternoon, after the attack, but neither had admitted to anything. This morning, Myra reported that Daniels had agreed to talk, but only to Valentin. She had refused to let me change his mind.

Imogen had spent a few hours in a hospital med chamber. Both Nikolas and Adams had disappeared, and no one knew if Adams still had Nikolas as a hostage. As far as missions went, it was something of a clusterfuck.

Valentin had tried to keep my involvement quiet, but that had lasted for all of two seconds. Now Kos citizens thought I was a bad queen, a traitor, *and* incompetent.

I'd suffered a major setback, but it wasn't a total loss. We'd captured two of the Quint soldiers. Myra wouldn't let me question them until Valentin was out of medical, which wouldn't be until tomorrow at the earliest.

But he wasn't sitting idle, even trapped in a med chamber. Yesterday, while we'd been attacking Adams, he'd had Myra question the young domestic affairs analyst who had paid Werner to disrupt my welcome dinner. Her picture was the only one that had matched the sketch.

Apparently she was so freaked out that she confessed as soon as Myra questioned her. *Hannah* had ordered her to find someone to cause a scene, not Asmo. It didn't make Hannah a traitor, not exactly, but it was another data point we could use.

And data was something I had plenty of, thanks to my information specialists. Last night, they'd come back with some financial irregularities for Lewis, Hannah, and Asmo, so I'd sent them digging deeper. Much to my annoyance, it seemed like Oskar was clean. But Myra was clean, too, so my gut instinct hadn't been entirely wrong.

Imogen had once again declined my offer to send her home, both last night and this morning. She trailed behind me as we made our way to Valentin's office, currently staffed only by his assistant, Lewis. His assistant who was taking money from Hannah Perkins.

I had the financial link, but now I needed to know the extent of the deal.

Myra met us outside the door. She had slipped out of medical yesterday afternoon, leaving Luka to watch over Valentin. I hadn't told her why I needed her presence, but based on her scowl, she'd guessed anyway. She gestured to the door. "Do you want me to come in with you?"

"No, I think he'll talk more if it's just me." He was also more likely to attack, but both Imogen and I were armed with electroshock pistols in addition to our plasma pistols. All of our weapons were concealed beneath our clothing. "Imogen has a camera, in case the surveillance goes down again."

"I'm linked in to the surveillance system, so yell if you need me. I've also activated neural link blocking in the whole office. He won't be able to link out, but neither will you."

I nodded and swept into the room. Lewis looked up from his desk. Surprise crossed his face before he smiled. "Queen Rani, it's good to see you again. How may I help you?"

He didn't look like a traitor. He appeared earnest and helpful, and his wholesome appearance made him seem trustworthy. He had worked for Valentin for years, and his betrayal was going to cut deep.

I fought to keep my expression pleasant as I dropped into the plush chair in front of his desk. "I'm hoping you can help me with some information. Hannah has spoken highly of you."

He froze, and his smile faded. "I don't know what you mean," he said stiffly.

"I don't have time to play coy. She told me about your arrangement and I want in." Lewis looked like he was going to protest again. I couldn't give him time to think. "I'm willing to pay double what Hannah's paying you, but only if I'm the sole recipient."

He looked stunned, then leaned forward and hissed, "You want me to turn on an imperial advisor. That's suicide. She'll expose me."

"She can't very well expose you without exposing herself, can she? I'm assuming you kept records?"

"What will you do with the information?"

I raised an eyebrow. "Does it matter? It won't be traceable back to you, if that's what you're worried about."

He thought about it for a second, and then his expression turned greedy. "I'll do it for triple."

"Valentin's schedule isn't worth that much to me." I waved a negligent hand. "I'm sure I can get it from someone else for less."

"You can't," he boasted. "His guard is fanatically loyal. And perhaps Hannah didn't tell you, but if you need the emperor to appear somewhere at a certain time, I can make it happen—for an additional fee, of course."

Fury pierced through my calm. This man was the reason Commander Adams had been able to capture Valentin in the first place, all those weeks ago. And Lewis hadn't stopped when he saw the result of his actions. He was the worst kind of traitor.

"He trusted you, you know," I said. "Why didn't you just ask him for help?"

Lewis blinked at the sudden switch, but then his face contorted in anger. "You conniving bitch."

"I don't think you're in any position to throw stones."

He lunged for something under his desk. I stood and drew my pistol in one smooth motion. Lewis didn't have time to do more than open his mouth before I shot him point-blank. He slumped in his chair, stunned.

I circled the desk and pressed an injector of sedative to his neck. Myra could stash him in a cell that prevented linking, but we couldn't risk him warning Hannah during the trip.

"He considered you a friend and you betrayed him." I leaned in close. "You are lucky that we might still need you, or I would not have used stun rounds. Try anything else, and a cell won't protect you. If you are very, very helpful, then I might look the other way when they release you in a decade or two. If not, I am a patient person, and I hold grudges *forever*."

The sedative took almost a minute to kick in, so he was able to hear every word while the stun round kept him paralyzed. I hoped it made a lasting impression.

Myra entered the office and stalked toward us. "Tell me it was highly satisfying to shoot him."

"It was," I agreed. "You have about twenty minutes to get him into an isolation cell before the sedative starts to wear off. Did the surveillance video catch everything he said?"

"Yes. I'll get him to the cell. I just hope I don't drop him down the stairs by accident. Where are you going?"

"As long as he lives, do what you will. I'm going to chat with Valentin's mother."

16

Unlike the last time I'd planned to visit Dowager Empress Marguerite Kos, this time I wore my usual clothes—black utility pants and a snug knit shirt. I had a knife tucked in my boot, but I'd left my pistols in my suite. Imogen looked as polished as usual, but I knew she was carrying at least four concealed weapons. She'd become paranoid, and I didn't blame her.

I rang the doorbell, and a few seconds later, Margie swung the door open. She had on a pair of soft, flowing black slacks and a gauzy orange shirt. She looked perfectly put together.

I'd asked her for a meeting without specifying why, and if she knew why I was here, she didn't show it. She smiled in greeting and didn't bat an eye at my unusual clothing choice. "Perfect timing, the food just arrived. I ordered brunch because I wasn't sure if you'd eaten yet."

I tried to bow to her, but she gathered me into a hug. It was so unexpected that I went rigid in surprise, then awkwardly patted her back. "Thank you for agreeing to see me."

"Of course!" She waved me in, then said, "Hello, Imogen. Welcome."

I didn't know where she'd learned my bodyguard's name, but Imogen's smile made it clear that it was a happy surprise.

"Thank you, Your Majesty."

"Please, call me Margie. Everyone does. Well, everyone I like." She winked at us. "Come in, come in. Rina, my guard, is waiting in the breakfast nook. I thought we'd be casual today, if that's okay with you."

"That suits me perfectly," I said.

Margie led us through a suite was that similar to mine, only on a much larger scale. The breakfast nook, despite its name, was a room as large as the dining room in my suite. It seemed to be designed for a long table that could seat eight or ten, but instead, a small circular table that seated four was at the far end, near the wall of glass leading to the balcony.

Place settings for two were laid out. Out near the balcony railing was another table with two more place settings. A beautiful woman with porcelain pale skin and strawberry blond hair sat at the table. She had a plasma pistol in a shoulder holster, so this must be Rina.

"I'd hoped we could talk in private," Margie said. "Imogen and Rina can eat on the balcony, where they can see but not hear. But I don't want you to be uncomfortable. We can bring them in if you prefer."

I, too, preferred to have this conversation in private, so this setup was ideal. I turned to Imogen. "Do you have any objections to being on the balcony?"

"May I check it first?"

When Margie nodded, Imogen stepped through the door. Rina stood and shook her hand. I couldn't even hear murmurs of their conversation, but then, I didn't have hearing augments. I wondered how effective the thick thermoplastic was at blocking sound for those with augments.

Imogen looked around, then came back in. "I don't have any objections. Thank you for ordering food for me."

Margie smiled. "I wasn't sure what either of you liked, so I ordered a variety of things. I hope you'll find something you enjoy."

"Thank you." Imogen bowed and retreated to the balcony.

Margie waved a hand at a delicate silver trolley laden with covered dishes. "I ordered family style. Grab your plate and help yourself." She demonstrated by doing exactly that.

I picked a fluffy omelet, some perfectly crisp potatoes, and a vibrant fruit salad. After a moment's debate, I added a layered pastry filled with chocolate. I bet Eddie and Zita would love to talk shop with the palace chefs.

I returned to the table, sat down, and tried to figure out how to broach a delicate subject without causing offense. Margie sat down across from me and gave me a shrewd look. "You have questions for me. I have questions for you. We can dance around each other with polite conversation, or we can cut the nonsense and get to the heart of the matter. Which do you prefer?"

I stared at her for a long second, trying to see exactly how honest she was being. Hopefully, she meant what she said. I asked the second most important question I had. "Which of your sons do you support as emperor?"

She sucked in a breath, then huffed out a rueful sound. "You don't pull your punches, do you?"

Considering I'd wanted to ask her about Nikolas's father and why she'd cheated on her husband, I thought I was being at least a little tactful. I hoped we'd get to that answer without me having to be so crass as to ask outright.

"The short answer is that I fully support Valentin. The long answer is very long indeed. Do you have designs on my son?"

I smiled to see she gave as good as she got. "I like Valentin and enjoy spending time with him, but he comes from generations of royalty while I'm a queen in name only, and barely that. It would never work." That came out far more bitter than I had intended, so I continued, "I promised him four weeks of my time to try to figure out which of his advisors want him dead. I'm paying that debt."

Something flashed across her face, too fast to catch, but she didn't interrupt. I ate slowly and mulled my next question. "Do you know where Nikolas has been hiding?"

Stark pain twisted her expression before she smoothed it away. "No." She sighed. "He is furious with me. I've tried to contact him every week since he stormed out, but he's ignored all of my messages. I'm afraid he is making bad choices. How much has Valentin told you?"

"He hasn't told me much. I know that everyone thought Nikolas would be the next emperor until Victor Kos died and left new instructions. Valentin told me the change was made because Nikolas wasn't Victor's son." I said it as gently as possible, but she still flinched. "It seems no one was particularly happy with the switch, and now people want Valentin dead."

"He trusts you far more than you think if he told you that much," she said quietly. She gazed at me for an eternal minute before seemingly coming to a decision. "I will tell you the whole story, but you must swear to never repeat it, not even to Valentin."

"You will have to explain why I can't tell Valentin before I'll agree to that promise."

She nodded thoughtfully. "That is fair. Valentin fiercely protects those he loves, even if doing so is to his detriment. I did not realize the threat against him was so dire until the attacks this week—he never told me, never even hinted at it. If you hadn't confirmed that you were here to find out who wanted him dead, I might've even written the attack off as Rogue rebels, as rumors indicate."

"You didn't know Valentin was being threatened?" I asked skeptically.

"Oh, I knew the Confederacy wanted him dead and had captured him, and I knew a few families next in line for succession would be happy if he died, but I didn't know we had active traitors in house. I've talked to him several times in the last few days and he hasn't mentioned it at all. When I asked who he thought was behind the attack, he blamed Quint and deftly changed the subject."

I blurted out my first thought. "He's going to kill me for telling you."

Margie chuckled, but she had steel in her tone when she said, "Not if I kill him first for keeping me in the dark, like I'm some useless old woman."

"I'm sure that's not why—"

She slashed a hand through the air. "My point stands. If you tell Valentin what I'm about to tell you, he will try to fix it, and he's already in a precarious position. So I'll have your promise."

"I promise I will not repeat it unless absolutely necessary to save your life or Valentin's."

"Or Nikolas's," she amended.

I had no love lost for Valentin's half-brother, but I nodded my acceptance anyway.

"Do you know how you can tell when someone is going to keep their word?" she asked. When I shrugged, she said, "They don't instantly agree to nonspecific, open-ended promises."

I could tell she was stalling, so I kept the conversation going to give her a bit more time. "Or maybe they are just very good liars." I toasted her with my chocolate pastry.

"Touché," she said with a grin.

She sobered and her expression went distant as she gathered herself to share what was an obviously painful story. "Victor and I had an arranged marriage that quickly turned into a love match. I was young when we were married, barely twenty, and far too naive. We tried for three years to have a baby because I knew my one job was to secure the line."

She must've seen the question on my face because she said, "Fertility procedures are not allowed for the Imperial line. It is seen as destiny if the ruling family cannot conceive naturally. And it is almost always followed by an 'accident' and a new emperor or empress in the form of whichever heir was next in line."

"That's the stupidest thing I've ever heard."

Her smile was grim. "I agree, and now, I would campaign to change the rules, but at the time, I was young and vulnerable. Victor's cousin Leo was part of the Imperial cabinet and fifth in line to the throne behind a bunch of healthy men and women—he knew he would never become emperor. He was fifteen years my senior and had the same good looks as Victor. He was also here all the time, while Victor was always off overseeing some war or treaty or something."

I doubted Valentin had two cousins named Leo, so I had the awful feeling that I knew where this story was going, but I held my peace.

Margie stared down at the table. "I loved my husband dearly and was deathly afraid of what would happen if I couldn't conceive. I confessed my worries to Leo. He told me that perhaps *Victor* was the one with the problem, not me. And he, being a good friend—or so I thought—offered me a solution. You can guess what it was."

I kept my expression perfectly blank as one of the puzzle pieces I was missing snapped into place, but anger burned in my belly. She'd been preyed on by an older man who had used her worry as a weapon against her, most likely to further his political goals.

"A few weeks later, Victor returned, and within a month, I was pregnant. I was blissfully happy and honestly thought it was Victor's child. I stopped seeing his cousin, and when it seemed like the rejection was going to be a problem, I had Victor reassign Leo to a diplomatic post. I thought that would be the end of it. As I said, I was young and dumb."

"You weren't dumb," I said. "You were manipulated."

"You are kind, but I made a mistake. I knew it was wrong. I hoped Victor would never find out, but I've found that secrets rarely stay buried. I don't know how he knew or when he learned Nikolas wasn't his. He never once mentioned it to me, and he treated Nikolas as if he were his own. When Valentin came along a year later as a happy surprise, Victor was elated, but he never favored Valentin over Nikolas."

"Why did Victor change the succession?"

"He didn't discuss it with me, so I can only guess." Margie paused and swallowed. She still wasn't meeting my eyes, and she was visibly uncomfortable.

"If it's too personal, you don't have to continue," I made myself offer, despite the fact that I desperately needed the confirmation.

A smile trembled on her mouth. "I didn't expect this to be so hard," she admitted.

I reached across the table and squeezed her hand. Her skin was clammy. The elegant empress was gone, and in her place was a woman swamped by pain and sorrow.

She took a steadying breath and continued, "Victor changed the succession two months before his death. Valentin said Victor's files revealed he knew about Nikolas from birth, though he had the DNA test sealed and struck from the record. He never told me about the test. He really did plan for Nikolas to be the heir."

"So why change it so late, when it would put both of his sons in an awkward position?"

Margie sighed. "I think someone found out and they were trying to blackmail Victor over Nikolas's illegitimate status. A late succession change would be difficult, but crowning an illegitimate son would be disastrous. I have no proof, but that is my gut feeling."

"Where is Nikolas's father now?" I asked quietly. I needed final proof before I went to Valentin with what I'd found.

Her short laugh was so bitter it hurt to hear. "The universe delivered my deepest shame directly to my doorstep, so I would never forget my biggest mistake. Leo is Hannah Perkins's husband."

It was the answer I'd expected, but hearing it confirmed was still a shock. "Why haven't you asked Valentin to send them away again? Sitting down at dinner next to them every night must be torture."

Her expression once again turned shrewd, but she didn't ask me how I'd known that Hannah and Leo had only returned to the palace full-time after the old emperor's death.

"The emperor doesn't have as much power as people believe, and that is doubly true for new emperors. Valentin is in an even trickier spot thanks to the last-minute succession change."

"You're protecting him, even though it's costing you," I breathed. "And yet you want to keep him in the dark because he would do the same for you. I wonder where he learned that tactic?"

Some of her spark returned. "I am his mother. It is my job to protect him, not the other way around."

17

I spent the rest of the day poring over the financial data I'd gotten from my contacts. They had given me raw data and flagged some initial places to look, but I liked to dig deeper myself. While I'd picked up the payments to Lewis fairly quickly because they were barely hidden, the rest of the money movement was harder to track.

Hannah and her husband owned a ridiculous number of companies, both on the books and off. Tracing money as it moved through the various accounts was time consuming and tedious, but it had to be done. Somewhere in here was the data I needed to prove that she was betraying Valentin.

I had a suite of software designed to sort through data like this, but without *Invictia*'s processing power, it was slow going. I felt the loss of my ship like the loss of a limb. I kept thinking I'd wake up and it would all be a nightmare, but it wasn't, and the grief snuck up on me in quiet moments.

Delving into the net while I waited for my queries to run, I found three kill contracts on Valentin, all opened within the past year. But no matter how I cross-referenced the payment amounts, I couldn't find the payments in any of Hannah's accounts.

But I did find matching amounts buried in an account owned by Copley Heavy Industries, Asmo's family's company. It was a tenuous link because the amount had been paid into a shell account. Once would've been a coincidence. Three times was not.

So, was Asmo working independently of Hannah, or were they working together? My gut said they were working together, but I hadn't found the link.

Imogen brought me dinner, and I ate while I worked. Valentin was due to be released tomorrow, and I wanted to bring him more than conjecture. As if my thoughts conjured him, he sent me a neural link request.

I briefly wondered if my thoughts *had* alerted him. Surely his abilities didn't extend that far, right?

I accepted the link. *You can't read my mind, can you?*

He laughed, and it was so good to hear that something loosened in my chest. *No. Were you thinking about me? Luka said you hadn't been by to bother him in a while, so I was worried about you.*

Yes, I was thinking about you. How are you feeling?

Better, but Junior won't let me out until tomorrow. He's driving me crazy. How are you?

I am okay. Busy. I'm digging through financials. It's super fun. I'm ready for you to be out so Myra will let me question the Quint soldiers we caught.

Yeah, she told me you were driving her crazy. She also told me about Lewis. His voice was flat, but I knew it had to hurt. *He's been with me for five years. I had no idea.*

I'm so sorry. I wish it had turned out to be Oskar. I wouldn't have minded taking that asshole down a few pegs.

Who else?

Hannah and Asmo.

He was quiet for a long time. *Do you know why?*

I'm still working on it. I hope to have an answer by tomorrow. And I really wanted to have this conversation in person because I knew that for all Valentin was pretending cool indifference, he had to be wounded and angry. I wanted to be able to wrap my arms around him and offer what comfort I could.

Be careful.

I will be.

He cut the link, and I was left with a mountain of data to sort through. It was going to be a long night.

———

IT HAD TAKEN HOURS, but I'd finally found the link between Asmo and Hannah, buried deep in their financial data. I'd barely been able to keep my eyes open, so I'd crashed just before dawn and had gotten a few hours of sleep.

Valentin was due to be released at noon. He was going to do a public appearance, then we were meeting in his suite, so I spent the morning going through all of the data my information specialist had found on Nikolas.

From what I could tell, Nikolas had been in Koan since he'd left the palace. His exact location was difficult to track because he wasn't paying rent or staying in hotels, which meant I had to guess his location based on the purchases he was making— including two yesterday morning.

By the time I'd tracked down what I thought was the likely building, I didn't have time to check out my hunch in person, which left me antsy. I hated incomplete data.

Ten minutes before Valentin and I were supposed to meet, I started pacing. Imogen watched me and rolled her eyes. "After all you've been through, now you're nervous?"

"I got his soldiers killed and didn't even catch the person responsible."

"Neither did the ten other people with you," Imogen reminded me gently. "I know you think you can do everything, but occasionally, you have to let the rest of us take our fair share of the blame."

She was technically right, but it didn't change how I felt. Valentin had already told me he didn't blame me, but it had been my call to attack Adams and my failure that had resulted in deaths. So I paced.

At two minutes to one, I headed for Valentin's suite. Luka opened the door, and my heart sank. If Valentin had been as eager to see me as I was him, wouldn't he have opened his own door?

"He's on the balcony. Imogen and I will be in the kitchen."

When I glanced at Imogen, her lip curled at the high-handed order, but she nodded her agreement.

I left them to it and made my way through Valentin's suite. It was even larger than Margie's and done in tasteful shades of blue and gray. The living room overlooked the balcony. Valentin stood staring out into the garden through the tall thermoplastic panels that had been added for extra protection. He wore a dark pinstriped suit that fit him perfectly, and the difference between us had never been more apparent.

I composed myself and pushed open the door to the balcony. Valentin turned as I approached, but I couldn't read his expression.

"How are you feeling?" I asked, just to break the awkward silence.

He closed the distance between us and pulled me into a tight hug. All of my careful planning went out the window, and I wrapped my arms around him.

"I was so worried," he murmured into my hair. "I've wanted to do this for two days."

"Me, too," I agreed. I enjoyed the moment before I remembered why he'd been in a med chamber to begin with. "I have more information about the traitors and Nikolas. I'm sorry I didn't get it fast enough to prevent the attack."

He chuckled but didn't let me go. "Only you would do something I've been trying to do for months in mere days and apologize for not doing it faster."

"I had help. And it wasn't cheap, FYI. I'm adding it to your bill. You might want to be sitting down when you look at it." I shut my mouth to stop the rambling.

He drew back far enough to meet my eyes. "Thank you." He slowly moved in, giving me plenty of time to back away. I stayed.

Valentin brushed his lips against mine. I closed my eyes and leaned into him. He kept the kiss light, but some of my tension melted. He was here, and he was okay. I didn't know what the future held for us, but for this moment, I enjoyed his mouth on mine, his hands holding me tight.

He pulled away, his reluctance clear. "As much as I would like to continue, I suppose work must come before play." He led me to a pair of outdoor chairs clustered around a little table. "Is this okay? Can I get you something to drink?"

"This is perfect, and I'm good." The nerves were back, and I just wanted this conversation to be over.

Valentin settled into the chair next to me. "You've been busy. I looked over the data you shared, but I want you to talk me through it, make sure I'm seeing the same things you are. And I would like to know where it came from."

"That one is easy, though I won't give you my exact sources. Suffice it to say that their job is digging up information that people would rather wasn't found. I've worked with them in the past."

"Before you became queen?"

That was a delicate way to ask if it was from the time I'd been working on kill contracts. "Yes."

"You trust them?"

I shrugged. "As much as I trust anyone. Their loyalty is to credits. I worked with the two of them independently and their data matched. I suppose there is a small chance they are both compromised and working together, but that would be unusual."

"I'm assuming they didn't obtain their information through legal channels?"

I laughed. "You assume correctly."

"Tell me what you found."

"As we discussed before, Hannah and Asmo are both working against you. Copley Heavy Industries, Asmo's family's company, nearly went under fourteen months ago, just before your father died. Only a large private loan from a shell company owned by Leo Perkins allowed them to remain solvent."

Valentin did not look surprised.

"I don't know why the original deal happened. Perhaps it was just good business. But then you became emperor instead of Nikolas, and suddenly, Hannah Perkins had a hold over Asmo. I believe she coerced him into helping her try to put Nikolas on the throne. Maybe he had his own reasons, too, but it's only after the loans that payments on three separate kill contracts on you came from deeply buried Copley accounts."

"Are you sure they are working together? Leo could have made a business decision without Hannah's involvement, and now it is just coincidence that she and Asmo are both betraying me."

"It's possible," I allowed. "I have enough evidence to prove their betrayal, but not that they are working together. If I could question one of them, then perhaps they would give up more information, but I didn't want to do that without your consent."

His expression hardened. "Both will be questioned. Extensively."

"As far as I can tell, Asmo has been dealing with the mercenaries and kill contracts, while Hannah is feeding both money and the information she got from your assistant to Commander Adams."

This time, true pain flashed on Valentin's face. "I still can't believe Lewis betrayed me."

"He apparently loves life's little luxuries and they don't come cheap. He needed additional income to keep living in the style to which he'd become accustomed. I don't have definitive proof yet that Hannah is the one providing the information to Adams, but she made additional payments to your assistant just before Adams picked you up last time. How many people knew exactly where you were going to be?"

Valentin closed his eyes. "Not many. It was a last-minute trip. Why does she hate me?"

"It's not you she hates, it's Quint. They killed her sons. She wants them wiped out and you are threatening peace. If Nikolas takes over, perhaps she thinks he's less likely to stop the war."

"She can't know that, though. Why risk it?"

I knew Valentin was too smart to accept half an answer. "I believe she knows or has proof that Nikolas is illegitimate and plans to blackmail him into continuing the war. And I believe she also promised Asmo that the war would continue to secure his help, since his family depends on the income from their shipbuilding company."

Valentin narrowed his eyes at me. "Why do you think she knows about Nikolas's parentage?"

"Because I spoke to your mother." Telling him that much

wasn't technically breaking my promise to Margie, and while I understood where she was coming from, I refused to lie to him. "That's all I can tell you."

Valentin shook his head. "I've long suspected Asmo, but Hannah was a surprise."

"You told me you didn't know who was betraying you!"

A chagrined smile touched the corners of his mouth. "I didn't, not for sure, and I didn't want my feelings to influence you." His smile died. "And I would've bet credits that Lewis was loyal."

I rubbed my face and prayed for patience. "Did you also know Nikolas has stayed in Koan since he left the palace?"

He blinked at me in surprise. "No."

"I was working on his location this morning, so I haven't had time to verify it, but his most recent transactions were yesterday near a building where Leo Perkins owns two penthouses."

"You got his recent transaction history? That would've taken me weeks of red tape. I was considering doing it anyway, but Mother kept thinking she could get him to come around and respond to our messages. I guess that didn't happen." Valentin laughed without humor and my heart ached for him. "You mentioned Leo owned the penthouses near there. Do you think Hannah has been helping Nikolas hide?"

"I would assume so."

"Mother is going to be crushed," he murmured. He shook his head and asked, "If Nikolas made purchases yesterday, did he escape or did Adams let him go?"

"My gut says he escaped. Even if they were working together at some point, I don't think Adams would've voluntarily let him go. Maybe Nikolas didn't know who Adams was, other than someone he was told would help 'reclaim' his throne, but Adams definitely knew who Nikolas was."

"Do you think they were working together?"

"Nikolas didn't have a break in his purchase history except for the morning after the attack on you, so he wasn't a captive for long, if at all. I think Adams used him until he wasn't useful anymore, then planned to keep him as a bargaining chip. We thwarted that plan when we attacked."

Valentin nodded. "I agree. I read Sakimoto's mission report. We need to speak to Daniels, but I think he helped Nikolas escape. It would've saved us all a lot of trouble if he had shot Adams instead of one of his flunkies, but I'm betting he hoped Lee would bag you and they could claim the promised reward. Trying to play both sides."

"Will Nikolas come after you on his own? Does he truly want you dead?"

Valentin slumped back in his chair and stared at the sky. "I found a snippet of video of the team who infiltrated the family wing. Nikolas was not with them. But if he was tortured, he could've given them codes that would've set off alarms. I think he would like me gone, but doesn't want to pull the trigger himself."

I squeezed his arm. What a terrible truth to learn about the older brother you'd looked up to for so many years. "What will you do now?"

He straightened in his seat. "I don't know. Despite Adams's attempts, we're both still alive, and we're about to cut off his money. Since it doesn't seem like Quint is supporting him directly, losing Hannah's financing will be a blow, and he'll be foaming at the mouth for revenge. If I could leak enough information to lead him into a trap, we could end him for good."

I considered the angles. "It's risky. Far better to figure out how Hannah was communicating with him and then use it yourself after shuffling her and Asmo off to an uncomfortable prison cell on a dark, cold planet."

"If only it were so easy," Valentin said with a sigh. "They've built up a lot of support, as evidenced by how fast the rumors of my death spread. They might be the only two actively betraying me right now, but they aren't the only two who would prefer Nikolas. It will have to be handled very carefully and the case must be airtight."

"I'm assuming you're already working on it with the information I sent you earlier?"

"I am," he agreed with a cunning smile. "I will take down Asmo first, as he actually made payments for the kill contracts. I know you only agreed to help me find the traitors and that debt is paid, but would you be willing to help me with Asmo anyway?"

"Well, I had initially planned to stay at least two weeks and Arx has survived without me so far, so I suppose I could find some time in my busy schedule to take down an asshole. And pick out my new ship, of course." I grinned. I didn't really expect him to replace *Invictia,* but I enjoyed teasing him.

His smile was like dawn breaking after a stormy night. "I already have some ship designs you might like, but the choice is yours. And thank you. Stay as long as you like."

"Tell me your plan."

He did, and it proved he knew exactly how to play the game.

18

Before we could deal with Hannah and Asmo, we had to deal with Lee, Daniels, and the two Quint soldiers. Valentin and I met Myra at the brig on the second level below the palace. It looked like someone had taken an old-fashioned stone dungeon and updated the cells with thermoplastic walls rather than bars.

"You didn't tell me you had a dungeon," I murmured.

Valentin laughed. "Truthfully, I'd forgotten what it looked like, but I used to play down here. You can see why."

Myra led us to a small interrogation room. Daniels was already seated inside, handcuffed to the chair. He looked young and nervous. His eyes flicked up to Valentin's face, then immediately dropped back to the table.

"I know where Nikolas is," he said quietly. "Let me go and I'll tell you."

"He's in a penthouse mid-city," Valentin said dismissively. Daniels looked up in shocked surprise. "You'll have to do better than that."

Daniels swallowed. "Lee was working with Hannah Perkins.

She thinks Nikolas is the true heir. I don't care one way or another, but I needed the money. I helped him escape Commander Adams. Please don't kill me."

"Tell us everything you know."

It wasn't much. Lee clearly hadn't trusted Daniels with important information. He only knew about Hannah because Lee had slipped up a few times and Daniels was observant, if nothing else.

Myra led him away, still pleading for his life.

Valentin sighed and rubbed his forehead. "Lee still refuses to talk, but Daniels's confession will be enough to prosecute her. They'll both be convicted of treason."

Myra returned before I could respond. "It's better if we question the Quints in their cells," she said. "Less risk of an incident." She didn't exactly look at me, but I knew precisely what she meant. These bastards had attacked us, blown up my ship, and nearly killed Valentin. They deserved what was coming to them.

The two Quint soldiers were separated, one at each end of the long hall. The first one sneered when he saw me. "How does it feel to be without a ship, bitch?"

Cold, hard fury made my voice sharp as glass. "Open the cell door."

"Absolutely not," Myra said.

"Can't touch me now," the red-haired man taunted. "I'm a political prisoner. I know my rights."

"Funny, there's no record of you in the system," Valentin said. "The sergeant major's report only mentioned the bodies we recovered. Yours was among them. We cremated the remains as per international treaty."

A flicker of doubt crossed the man's face. "You can't do that."

"I can and I did. Talk fast or I'm going to let Queen Rani in there with you."

Anticipation carved my smile into a thing of terrifying beauty.

Rationally, I hoped he gave us the information we needed. But personally, I hoped he held out and needed to be persuaded.

The man's ruddy skin paled until his freckles stood out. He backed away from the thermoplastic. "It wasn't me! I didn't attack your ship. You already killed one of the poor bastards who did. And you have Martin, right? Take your anger out on him."

Myra didn't let me into either soldier's cell, despite the fact that Martin as much as confessed to blowing up my ship. They *were* political prisoners, and returning them to Quint for prosecution would be a token of goodwill between Kos and Quint.

I knew it, but I didn't like it. At least one of the bastards responsible was already dead. And Valentin assured me that he would press the Quint Chairwoman for treason verdicts and capital punishment.

Valentin dismissed Myra with orders to let him know if anything changed. She eyed him, but didn't comment. Once she was out of sight, he led me back toward Martin's cell. "You have thirty seconds. Don't break him."

He stopped out of sight of the cell and handed me the key to the door. He had just delivered a present better than all my holidays combined. He understood my need for vengeance, but trusted that I wouldn't take it too far.

He understood *me*.

I brushed my lips across his. "Thank you."

———

I HADN'T EXPECTED Valentin's grand plan to require me to put on a gown, go to dinner, and make nice with the people who wanted him dead, but after we returned from the dungeon, I'd done exactly that. The gown was a gorgeous strapless scarlet affair that I adored. And it had certainly eased some of my worries when Valentin had been rendered mute at the sight of it.

But now, in the glitter of the ballroom, surrounded by fake smiles and suspicious glances, I just wanted tonight to be over with. Successfully.

Valentin and Margie were both in attendance, as were all of the advisors and Valentin's court. Valentin had escorted me around until a few minutes ago, when he'd quietly excused himself to go talk to a man old enough to be his grandfather.

Left alone with Imogen, I quietly drifted, playing shiny red bait.

It did not take Asmo long to find me.

He had on a light gray suit, and his expression was predatory. "Is it true that you nearly got Valentin's heir killed?" he asked without preamble.

"I was trying to rescue the idiot. He nearly got himself killed." Unlike Lewis, Asmo was a consummate politician. He was unlikely to reveal anything, no matter how I baited him. So I was going for a far more straightforward approach. Both Imogen and I wore hidden cameras. Mine was concealed in the heavy onyx necklace draped across my collarbones.

His mouth curled into a sly grin. "That's not what I heard."

I took his arm, despite the fact that his touch made my skin crawl. "Speaking of rumors, I heard an interesting one."

"Oh? Do tell."

I led him to the edge of the room, to an empty little alcove. Imogen stood behind us, both blocking us from view and blocking Asmo's escape route. She had been less than enthused with this plan, but she was playing her part. When I turned to Asmo, he leaned in with a knowing leer, then frowned when I stepped back.

Hoping to keep him off balance, I tilted my head to the side and said, "I heard a rumor that a certain shipbuilding company paid for three kill contracts on Emperor Kos."

If I hadn't caught the split-second of shock in his eyes, I would have thought he hadn't heard me. His expression gave almost nothing away. "You heard lies."

"One would hope, but no. I have proof. What I do with that proof remains to be seen."

"Good luck proving a lie." He turned to leave, but Imogen's plasma pistol changed his mind.

"Shout for the guards and your downfall will be a lot more public, because they've already been informed to arrest you at the slightest provocation. Imogen, too, wouldn't mind shooting you, so keep your hands visible."

He turned back to me with a furious expression. "What is the meaning of this?"

"I'm giving you a chance to bargain for your life. Privately."

"I'm supposed to believe that you would let me go?"

My smile was not kind. "No. You've made your bed. But if you can convince me that you acted alone, I won't go after your sister and your family. And don't bother contacting them, they're already in protective custody."

He flinched as the shot landed true. I wasn't sure that he had an altruistic bone in his body, but he did seem to care about his sister. His mouth twisted into a snarl. "You're working with Valentin."

"Yes."

"What do you want?"

"Everything you have on Hannah Perkins."

I'd once again shocked him, but he hid it behind a crafty smile. "What makes you think I know anything about Advisor Perkins?"

I shrugged. "If that's how you want to play this, protective custody can turn into real custody in the blink of an eye. And we have more than enough evidence to convict your entire family and execute them as traitors to the Empire. I don't need you, but you very much need me. I was the one who persuaded Valentin that your knowledge might be worth your life."

"I want amnesty for me and my family."

"And I want a million credits and universal peace, but we don't always get what we want. If you acted alone, your family will get amnesty. You will get your life. If you are extremely helpful, that life could include a very posh cell. If not, well, I'm sure you've heard the prison horror stories."

"You are a cold bitch."

My smile was all teeth. "I am the cold bitch who has your sister. You tried to kill someone important to me. Do you really think that I wouldn't return the favor, given even the slightest cause?"

"This was all Hannah's fault. I didn't want to do it, but she blackmailed me. I shouldn't have to pay for her treachery."

I wanted to roll my eyes, but instead I kept my expression earnest. "Make your case well enough and perhaps Valentin will agree."

"Fine, I will tell you what I know. After I have a signed pardon for my family."

"Done." I led him through a side door. It would look to the room like I'd just left Valentin for his advisor, but it couldn't be helped. Natalie Sakimoto waited in the service hallway beyond with three additional soldiers.

While Asmo was still busy scowling at Natalie, I injected him with the same sedative I'd given Lewis. He whirled on me. "We had a deal."

"We still do. This is just a little insurance that you'll make it to your cell without any outside interference."

He threw a clumsy punch at me. I caught his fist and squeezed.

"You don't need working hands to talk, so tread lightly." When he winced in pain, I let go.

Natalie cuffed him and waited until he wilted to the floor before picking him up. "We'll get him to his new accommodations, don't worry," she said.

Once they were gone, Imogen turned to me. "Do you think he'll cooperate?"

"He will once he realizes he's out of options. I wouldn't have believed it if I hadn't seen it, but his sister's life is an effective lever."

"Do you think he has dirt on Hannah?"

"Yes. I think he's too smart not to have kept copies of everything."

"I hope you're right."

———

I LINKED Valentin to let him know that the first part of the plan had been successful, then I waited ten minutes before returning to the ballroom. My disappearance hadn't gone unremarked. Valentin made a point of looking directly at me, then turning and speaking to Margie, giving me his back.

It was a snub, and not a subtle one. A twitter ran through the crowd as everyone tried to figure out what I'd done with Asmo and why I'd come back alone. Guards were on alert in case Hannah decided to bolt, but Valentin expected her to approach me.

I was on my second circuit of the room when Hannah's curiosity got the better of her. She had on a midnight blue dress, and her husband wasn't with her.

"What did you do to Asmo?"

I looked around, as if I expected to see him. "Nothing. Why do you ask?"

"Don't play dumb with me. The entire ballroom saw you leave with him and return alone. Do I need to involve the guards?"

I let myself imagine that hilarious scenario for a couple seconds and smiled. "I don't think that's necessary." I gave her an appraising look. "In fact, we had a very interesting conversation."

Her mouth pinched like she'd bitten into a lemon. "What could you possibly have to discuss?"

"You, actually. He was quite talkative."

She was wily and wasn't going to go down so easily. "Asmo talks a lot and says little."

I laughed. She might be a horrible person, but she had Asmo's number. "True, but in this case, he has proof to back up his words."

"You might have gained Asmo's support, but you've lost Valentin's. Anything you think you know is worthless."

"Maybe, maybe not. I don't need Valentin to achieve my goal." I turned to leave, and she grabbed my arm.

Imogen stepped up beside me. "Unhand Queen Rani."

"Call off your dog," Hannah demanded, "and tell me what you want."

"I want Adams. He attacked Arx and destroyed my ship."

Surprise flashed across her expression before she smoothed it over into a polite mask. "Perhaps I could assist you after all. I have many diplomatic connections. I could send him a message."

"Do it, and I'll forget what Asmo told me. I don't care about your petty political squabbles. I want the man who hurt my people."

She nodded. "Consider it done. Send me the message you want me to pass along, and I'll see what I can do."

Her smile looked a lot like victory. She just didn't know whose victory she was celebrating.

———

DINNER HAD DRAGGED on forever while Valentin and I had pretended to be at odds. Oskar had outdone himself with sly, snippy comments, and I had never been so glad to see dessert. I'd escaped as soon as was polite and sought refuge in my suite.

I stripped off my beautiful gown and careful makeup and made my way to Valentin's suite. But now that I stood outside his door in my pajamas and bare feet, I hesitated. We were supposed to talk, but the last time we'd tried an after dinner talk, I'd jumped him, and then my ship had exploded, so our track record wasn't exactly great.

I hadn't yet knocked, but the door swung open. Valentin also wore pajamas. "It would've been more gentlemanly to pretend I didn't know you were there, to let you decide on your own. But I wanted to tip the scales in my favor." He grinned. "Is it working?"

I smiled at him. "Yes."

He stepped aside to let me enter, then led me to the living room. Two glasses and a decanter of red wine waited on the end table.

"I have whisky, too, if you would prefer it."

"No, wine is perfect."

I accepted a glass and settled on the sofa. This reminded me of the last time we'd tried this, both the good and the bad. Soon, I would need to make plans to salvage *Invictia*'s remains. The loss broke my heart.

After Adams had blown up the warehouse and disappeared, Valentin had posted a huge bounty on him. Every hunter in the city would be looking for him, but since he hadn't been found, we assumed he had already fled off-planet. Maybe we could make it through the evening without anything else blowing up.

Valentin picked me up, sat down, and tucked me into his lap. His strength reminded me of the muscles hiding under his clothes —and how those muscles had felt under my hands.

When I remained silent, he quietly asked, "Are you uncomfortable?"

"No. In fact, I was imagining you naked."

He choked on his wine. Good to know I could still surprise him. I set aside both glasses and patted his chest while he caught his breath. He trapped my hand beneath his, pressed against his heart. We were close enough that I could see the dark flecks in his gray eyes.

"Stay," he whispered.

"I already agreed to stay for a while," I murmured, unsure what he was asking.

"Stay with me. Permanently."

I didn't expect the sharp stab of yearning. Home was something I'd craved for a long, long time. I knew I couldn't accept, but curiosity made me ask, "As what? Your guest? Your mistress? An exiled queen in need of assistance?"

"As whatever you'd like."

"And what happens when you have to get married?"

"Then I hope you'll say yes."

Every cell in my body froze. "Are you asking me to marry you?"

His smile was so tender it hurt. "No, it's too soon, as evidenced by you turning to stone in my arms."

My emotions were in a jumble that I couldn't begin to sort out. "But you hardly know me."

"I know enough."

Bitter laughter bubbled up. "You really, really don't. I joined a mercenary squad at ten. By fifteen, I was a proficient killer. I earned enough credits to buy my augments and my own ship by twenty. By the time I quit at twenty-five, I'd become a legend in the elite merc circles. I've lost track of the number of people I've killed, and I regret many of their deaths. My soul is stained with blood."

"You're the Golden Dahlia. I know."

I met his eyes, but I didn't see condemnation. "How?"

"I saw you give the card to Finlay and caught his message."

"That *was* you I saw in the bar that night. That was a stupid risk. Did you think Luka would betray me? Were you only at Blind?"

"No, I trust Luka. He would've protected you as well as he protects me, but I wanted to be nearby in case you ran into more trouble than the two of you could handle." He chuckled. "Of course that would likely take an armored assault vehicle guarded by two platoons of berserkers. I followed you to the other two bars, but I ditched the coat for a hat and balaclava. You almost caught me when you circled back."

"Does Luka know you were out?"

"He might've caught me outside Blind. Then I had to listen to him yell at me all night via neural link."

I kind of agreed with Luka, not that I would ever tell him. But Valentin was trying to distract me, and I needed him to understand what being the Golden Dahlia really meant. "I killed people for money, and while I wouldn't say I enjoyed it exactly, I liked the challenge and I loved the money. There is no rosy side here. When I could afford to be picky, I tried to ensure the targets deserved what they were getting, but there were times when I couldn't."

"I killed as a soldier, and then as I climbed into command, I ordered soldiers into battles I knew they couldn't win, just to buy the rest of the fleet more time. You may have killed individuals or even small groups, but I've killed battalions for a rock neither side needed."

"War is different."

"It's not," he said, very quietly.

"Even if I wanted to stay,"—and it was so, *so* tempting—"I have a responsibility to my people. I can't abandon them. The war between you and Quint has already cost them their homes. The Rogue Coalition was their last hope. I won't take away that hope."

"I know. It was a selfish request. But what if the war were over? And we split time between here and there?"

I looked at him in surprise. "You would be willing to live part-time in Arx?"

"After the war is over, yes. Like you, I can't abandon my people when they need me."

Cautious hope bloomed. "In that case, once the war is over, I'm willing to try."

His thumb brushed my jaw. "Then I will end the war." He said it with such certainty that I believed he could do it. The hope grew roots and burrowed into my heart. A happy, buoyant smile broke across my face.

He matched my smile and sealed the promise with a kiss that threatened to send me up in flames. Before I could lose my mind, I broke away with a groan. Valentin had just been let out of medical earlier today, after a grievous injury. "Did Junior clear you for strenuous activity?"

I could tell from his face that he wanted to lie, but he sighed and shook his head.

"How long?"

"A week, but I feel fine." He gave me a wicked smile. "And this isn't strenuous; I'm just sitting here." I pressed my hand to his chest and felt his heart racing. When I quirked an eyebrow at him, he grinned. "He didn't mention anything about heart rate."

I kissed him gently, to comfort rather than entice. "I just got you back. I don't want to lose you again."

He gathered me close and pressed a kiss to my temple. "You won't," he promised.

I planned to hold him to that promise.

EPILOGUE

When Asmo realized how much data we had on him, he sang like a bird. And he had a lot of evidence of Hannah's treachery, all carefully documented. Prison was too good for him, but Valentin felt like he had to keep his word.

I had no such compunction where traitors were concerned, but no one asked me.

Hannah sent my message to Adams the day after I talked to her at dinner. She sent me a confirmation with a meeting time and location a month from now. I suppose she'd thought that she could get two loose ends to solve themselves, but all she'd done was give Valentin more evidence against her. She and her husband were both arrested.

Asmo's trial went off without a hitch, exactly a week after I'd first arrived in Koan. Despite Valentin's complaints about red tape, he could make things happen quickly when he was determined.

The tribunal found Asmo guilty of high treason and sentenced him to life in prison. His sister and his family's company were left alone, but Valentin assured me that he had them all under heavy surveillance.

Hannah's trial was the next day, a week after the attack on Valentin, and the tribunal was not as forgiving. She tried to sway them to her side with threats and ultimatums, but the tribunal wasn't having it. Both she and Leo were convicted of high treason and conspiracy to commit murder. They were sentenced to death, the first capital punishment in the Kos Empire in more than a century.

Lee and Daniels were scheduled for a special military tribunal next week. Valentin did not expect their cases to have any surprises. Lee still hadn't confessed or spoken to anyone at all, but a review of her finances showed the payments from Hannah.

Nikolas remained in Koan. I'd given Margie his location and she'd gone to see him twice a day until he'd finally let her in. She refused to talk about it, but I hoped she was making progress. If Nikolas really had been working with Hannah and Asmo, then his life was about to get far more difficult without his allies.

Commander Adams had disappeared. With the bounty Valentin had posted, he wouldn't find any refuge in Kos space, and I also had my own people looking for him. So far, he remained a ghost, but I held out hope that he would actually show at the meeting Hannah had arranged, even though we both knew it was a trap.

Meanwhile, Valentin kept working on the peace treaty with Quint. He had returned the two captured soldiers, much to Chairwoman Soteras's delight. She had promised they would receive swift justice. It would likely take a year or more to hammer out all of the treaty details. Adams was obviously against peace and had enough influence to become a problem, so he would need to be dealt with before he could derail the entire treaty.

I'd done as much as I could in Koan, so I reluctantly returned to Arx to prepare for my next hunt. I hated to leave before Valentin's week-long strenuous activity ban was up, but the faster I dealt with Adams, the faster our future would be safe.

And I was not going to let some asshole who couldn't accept defeat steal my future happiness.

Commander Adams's days were numbered.

EXCERPT FROM AURORA BLAZING

**Read on for a sneak peek at
Jessie Mihalik's next romantic science fiction novel,
Aurora Blazing
Available in October 2019 from Harper Voyager!**

————

CHAPTER ONE

Lady Taylor had bugs in her walls and not the kind with jointed legs and crunchy bodies. The tortured piano in the corner whined out something that vaguely resembled music as I fought the urge to pull out my com and track the signals to their sources. Three different broadcast frequencies meant at least three different agencies were interested in what happened at a Consortium ladies' afternoon tea.

Or perhaps they were just interested in Lady Taylor.

My mind spun down that avenue, looking for motive, before I

forcefully reined it in. I had to focus, dammit. If only these events weren't so dreadfully dull.

A nearby conversation caught my attention. I smiled into my teacup as the two girls behind me debated in fierce, heated whispers whether or not I'd killed my husband. They didn't realize the terrible piano music wouldn't hide their discussion.

My youngest sister stiffened at my side as she overheard a particularly exuberant theory. I put a restraining hand on her arm. Catarina's eyes flashed with fury, but I minutely shook my head and she settled down. She glanced behind us, no doubt cataloging the girls' faces for future retribution.

Neither the words nor the speculation bothered me, and indeed, they gave me something to focus on. But my youngest sister had always chafed at the daily viciousness of Consortium life.

A quick glance confirmed the girls were from one of the lower houses. A brunette with straight hair, tan skin, and a face just a touch too narrow for true beauty sat beside a stunning young woman with ebony skin and black curls. We had been introduced at some point, but memory was fluid and mine more than most. I couldn't recall either of their names.

This was likely their first social season—they hadn't yet learned how to subtly skewer an opponent with a smile and a few well-chosen words. Even Catarina could probably send them from the room in tears with little more than a sentence.

Besides, the girls' speculation as to *how* I could've killed Gregory provided some much-needed distraction. The formal sitting room was almost claustrophobically small, with no windows and heavy, ornate furniture. You'd never know we were in the penthouse of a thirty-story building.

The two dozen impeccably dressed, sharp-eyed women seated

in little cliques facing the piano only added to the oppressive atmosphere.

"Bianca, why do you let them continue?" Cat asked in an exasperated whisper. I'd been on the receiving end of many exasperated whispers lately.

"What, you don't think I paid Gregory's mistress to get him drunk and push him down the stairs?" I asked, quoting the latest ridiculous suggestion.

Uncertainty flashed across her face as her mask slipped the tiniest bit. "Of course not," she said stoutly. She shot me a sly smile and continued, "You're a von Hasenberg—you'd do it yourself."

That was as close as any of my sisters ever got to asking me what had really happened. And every time it caused a riot of emotions—fear, anger, relief, love—as I waited to see if *this time* would be the time they would ask.

I set my teacup on its saucer with precise, iron-willed control. The two pieces met without the telltale rattle that would indicate my internal turmoil. The interminable piano piece finally came to an end, saving me from having to respond.

"—was poison—" the curly-haired gossip said into the sudden silence. She choked off the words on a strangled gasp. Out of the corner of my eye, I saw her freeze as every person in the room turned her way. Her black curls trembled as she swallowed nervously. The sharks paused, smelling blood.

"What was that, dear?" Lady Taylor asked with false sweetness. She had a daughter—one who could not play the piano for love or money. If these two were shunned, her daughter would have a better shot at making a good match.

The silence stretched as the girl floundered. The second girl, the brunette, sat stone-still, doing her best to blend in to the furniture.

"She was asking if poison was the best option to remove a particularly stubborn weed," I said smoothly. Lady Taylor's laser gaze swiveled to me, but as the daughter of a High House, I outranked her, and she knew it.

"Is that so?" she asked.

I tipped up my chin a fraction. Ice frosted my tone. "You doubt my word?" When she took a second too long to answer, I stood. Catarina rose with me.

Lady Taylor paled beneath her flawless makeup as all eyes now focused on her. "Of course I didn't mean—"

I would feel sympathetic, except she *had* meant to cause offense. She was conniving, and I'd let her get away with too much for too long because I just didn't care. I'd already done my duty to my House, my position was secure, and I had no one I needed to impress.

But the moment she'd doubted my word, she'd taken it too far, a fact that was just now dawning on her.

"I realized I have somewhere else to be," I said. I turned to the curly-haired gossip. She was as young as I expected, perhaps seventeen or eighteen. "Walk with me," I said.

She rose but kept her head bowed. When the brunette started to rise, too, I shot her a quelling glare. She wilted back into her seat. She hadn't attempted to bail her friend out, so she would have to fend off the sharks on her own.

I linked arms with the curly-haired girl and swept from the room over the protests of Lady Taylor. Catarina kept pace beside me. We didn't speak until we'd cleared the front door.

"My lady, I'm *so* sorry," the girl said miserably as I pulled her along toward the transport platform.

"You should be," Catarina said.

I rolled my eyes. "What is your name?" I asked.

"Lynn Segura, second daughter of House Segura," she said.

House Segura was a small House with modest assets, one of the many lower houses that made up the bulk of the Royal Consortium. "How did you manage an invite to Lady Taylor's tea?" I asked. House Taylor was one of the more powerful lower houses.

"Chloe received an invite and brought me along," she said. At my blank look, she blushed and elaborated, "Chloe Patel, first daughter of House Patel. She is the woman I was with."

That made more sense. House Patel was also a lower house, but they had three eligible sons around the same age as Lady Taylor's daughter. And their interests dovetailed nicely with House Taylor's.

"Are you going to tell my father?" Lynn asked.

We emerged outside into the sun. The transport platform had tall glass panels to block the worst of the wind, but a breeze swirled gently, teasing the hem of my gray dress. Serenity sparkled under the cloudless sky. The only city on Earth and the heart of the Royal Consortium, Serenity was a hive of activity. Transports and ships crisscrossed the sky, glittering like jewels.

For all its flaws, I loved this city.

I let the girl fret in silence while the three of us climbed into the waiting House von Hasenberg transport. Catarina sat facing backward while I sat next to Lynn. I waved the embedded chip in my left arm over the reader. "Take us to Macall's Coffee House," I said. The transport chimed its acceptance, then slid off the thirtieth-floor platform and headed northwest.

The glass panel in the floor showed another transport in House von Hasenberg colors—black and gold—shadowing us from below. Our security detail was a new and unwelcome change, but three weeks ago we'd gone to war with House Rockhurst, so it was deemed a necessary evil.

If the ladies of the House hadn't presented a united front, we would have had armed guards escorting us to tea. As it was, they escorted us to evening events, but only followed us via transport during the day. Serenity was officially neutral ground, but both Father and our director of security were paranoid.

Lynn practically vibrated in her seat, desperate to know if I'd tell her father but smart enough not to ask again. She had potential.

"I am not going to tell anyone," I said. "We are going to enjoy a cup of coffee in public and have a nice chat, then we will part on agreeable terms. The next time I see you, I will make a point of saying hello."

Lynn's eyes narrowed. "Why?" she asked.

"Because your behavior made a boring tea interesting. And because if I do not, Lady Taylor will destroy you."

Lynn flinched as the full implication of her actions hit her. She squared her shoulders and met my eyes. "What can I do to repay you?"

I tilted my head as I regarded her. I'd saved her because I could and because I remembered my own disastrous first season. I hadn't expected anything in return, but I wasn't so hasty as to turn down a debt freely offered, either. She wasn't the first girl I'd saved, and thanks to that, I had eyes in many places.

"You do not *have* to do anything," I said seriously, "but if you ever overhear anything you think I might find interesting, I would be grateful if you would let me know."

She nodded, her eyes bright. "Consider it done."

———

Macall's Coffee House occupied a ground-floor corner of a tall office building in Sector Three of the von Hasenberg quarter.

Floor-to-ceiling windows wrapped around two sides of the shop, giving those inside a sense of airy lightness.

The cafe was decorated in cream and brown, with real wood and leather furniture—no plastech dared to breach these walls. The tables and chairs were beautifully mismatched with charming, understated elegance. Someone had put a lot of time and effort into making the design look effortless.

House von Hasenberg retained a table with an ideal location: next to the window and slightly separate from the surrounding tables. All three High Houses retained tables, aware that as much business happened here as on the floor of the Royal Consortium. But because we were in the von Hasenberg quarter, our House had received the best location.

After the waiter left with our orders, I activated the silencer built into the table—another perk. By default, silencers only blocked sound in one direction, so we could still hear the people murmuring around us, but no one could eavesdrop on our conversation.

The silencer prevented any sounds or wireless signals in a two-meter radius from transmitting outside that radius, including voices, coms, or bugs. If someone wanted to know what we were gossiping about, they'd have to read our lips.

Once Lynn realized I really wasn't going to bite, her wit and humor returned. She wasn't quite brave enough to ask me outright if I'd killed my husband, but the same cleverness that made her spout wild theories made chatting with her entertaining. Saving her had been the right move.

We chatted for forty-five minutes before Lynn took her leave. The door had barely closed behind her when Catarina pinned me with a stare. "This is how you know everything about everyone," she said. "You have a legion of spies masquerading as young women."

I sipped my lemonade and said nothing. She was wrong, but she drew the exact conclusion I had intended. Shame slid through my system, soft and sour. I didn't like lying to family, even by omission, but it was the only way to ensure they—and I—stayed safe.

"How many have you saved?" Cat asked.

"I don't keep track. A dozen, maybe. I started when I returned home after Gregory's death." The true number was twenty-seven, and that only counted the people I'd truly helped, not those like Lynn who had just needed a momentary rescue. If I included everyone, the number would be closer to sixty. And I'd started well before Gregory's death.

Our prenup had protected House von Hasenberg's interests, not mine. When my husband died, I inherited nothing. His family wasted no time hustling me out of their lives. Money was far less of an issue than stability and familiarity, so I ran home like the wounded animal I was.

"I can't believe you're running your own spy ring," Catarina said with a laugh. "I bet it drives Ian insane."

I smiled. Ian Bishop was the director of House von Hasenberg security—an inconspicuous title for a far-reaching power. He had his fingers in House intelligence gathering, security forces, and even military maneuvers. He was the most arrogant man I'd ever met, and that was saying something considering I grew up in a High House.

He was also one of the most handsome, but a trained interrogator couldn't force the admission from my lips.

One of my few true pleasures these days was beating Ian to a piece of intelligence. It had turned into something of a competition, and I was currently ahead by two. Or, at least, my shadowy, anonymous online persona was. Ian had no idea I was feeding him information from multiple directions.

"Ian doesn't think the daughter of a High House is capable of anything other than being a trophy wife," I said. "I enjoy proving him wrong."

"I thought Ada would've disabused him of that notion," Catarina said. "He tried to catch her for two years and failed."

My younger sister Ada was exceptional, but even she wasn't *that* good—as head of security for a High House, Ian had nearly infinite resources at his disposal. He'd failed because I'd fed him a constant stream of false information, while giving Ada all the info she needed to stay ahead of him.

I wanted to tell Cat, to let her in on the secret, but one secret led to twenty others, each more dangerous than the last. I held my tongue.

"Oh, I'm supposed to meet Lady Ying in twenty minutes to go shopping. You want to join?" Catarina asked.

I repressed a shudder. Shopping with Catarina was a masochistic endeavor if ever there was one. The girl could spend seven hours in a single store. Seven. Hours.

Luckily for the rest of us, Ying Yamado was always game for a shopping trip. She and Catarina were close friends—as close as the daughters of two High Houses could be, at least.

"I'll pass, thanks. I'd like to make it home before tomorrow," I said.

Catarina rolled her eyes at me. "I'm not *that* bad."

I just raised my eyebrows until she cracked and broke down into giggles.

"Okay, maybe I am. But you're missing out," she said as she stood. She kissed the air next to my cheek and then she was gone. I disabled the silencer, and the communication signals around me rushed in, overwhelming and nauseating.

After all of this time, I should be used to it, but Gregory's gift just kept on giving. He'd been a brilliant scientist and a horrible husband, wrapped together with a morally bankrupt bow. I don't think it ever occurred to him to *not* experiment on me.

Now I could mentally intercept and decrypt wireless signals, whether I wanted to or not, and I had no idea how. Gregory's lab had been destroyed, taking most of his secrets to the grave.

He had tampered with both my brain and my nanobots, the infinitesimal robots in my blood that were supposed to aid healing. Father would dearly love the tech, so much so that he would absolutely approve more experiments on me if he found out about my abilities.

I'd been a test subject for long enough.

So I kept my secrets to myself and became a grieving widow in public. It kept Father from pushing me to remarry—which I would never do—and covered some of my new eccentricities.

I attended teas and lunches and balls when I would've preferred staying home. But staying home would not let me find other young women who could use my help, so I sucked it up and played the idle aristocrat.

At home, I earned my keep by using my network to track down information for House von Hasenberg. Father didn't know exactly where my information came from, but he knew that if he needed something found, I could find it.

I finished my lemonade and pretended my head didn't feel like it was being stabbed with stilettos. The headaches were worse when I was in an open public space, as my piddly human brain couldn't keep up with all of the information flowing to the implant from my modified nanos.

My com lit up in my mind's eye a second before it vibrated in my handbag. Because I was attuned to it, I knew I'd received a message and what it said without looking at the device itself. Decoding transmissions, even the secure transmissions my com received, was almost comically easy. Whatever else Gregory had been, he truly had been a gifted scientist.

I'd taught myself to tune out most transmissions so they became ignorable background noise. It didn't help with the headaches, but at least I didn't have to constantly hear strangers' messages in my head all day. Now they burbled along like a distant stream in the back of my mind. I could hear individual messages if I focused, but mostly they were white noise.

I was Gregory's fantasy of an ideal wife, forced to listen to everything without being able to respond. I didn't know if he'd planned to add transmission abilities later or if he'd designed it this way as a cosmic joke. If it was the latter, the joke was very much on him. I smiled in grim satisfaction.

I pulled out my com to read and respond the old-fashioned way. The message was from Ian. It was short and to the point. *You were scheduled to return home, not split from your sister. The security detail followed her. Remain where you are until the replacement detail arrives. I have eyes on you until then.*

My smile morphed into a grin as I typed my reply. *I was just leaving. I'll be home before they arrive.*

STAY PUT. The reply was so fast, I wondered if he had pretyped it. I'd hate to think I was so predictable.

I didn't bother with a reply. If he was actually monitoring the cameras, he'd see me leave. Otherwise, he'd certainly notice when my tracker started moving. Either way, I wasn't going to sit around for who knew how long waiting for his security team. My head ached at just the thought.

The coffee shop was close enough that I could walk home, but that was sure to make Ian apoplectic. And while I didn't really think Serenity was unsafe, we *were* at war and some basic safety precautions were prudent.

I ordered a House transport and waited until it arrived before leaving the building. I didn't see Ian's second security detail, so he was sure to be livid. I resisted the urge to tap into our House security cameras to see for myself.

The transport dropped me at the private family entrance without incident. I cleared the new security checkpoint then waved my embedded identity chip over the reader at the door. The reader beeped as it verified that my chip and biometrics matched. The door opened, and I let myself into the ornately carved stone building I'd called home for twenty-one of my twenty-five years.

The heavy stone blocked some of the wireless signals, and I sighed in relief. I stepped out of the entryway and a shadow detached itself from the draperies.

I had a blaster in hand before my brain recognized that I wasn't being attacked by a stranger. No, I was being stalked by Ian Bishop.

I wasn't sure that was an improvement.

———

Preorder Aurora Blazing today!

ABOUT THE AUTHOR

Jessie Mihalik has a degree in Computer Science and a love of all things geeky. A software engineer by trade, Jessie now writes full time from her home in Texas. When she's not writing, she can be found playing co-op video games with her husband, trying out new board games, or reading books pulled from her overflowing bookshelves.

CONNECT WITH JESSIE:

www.jessiemihalik.com
Twitter: @jessiemihalik
Facebook: /JessMihalik
Instagram: @jessmihalik
Want all of the latest book news, info, and snippets delivered straight to your inbox? Sign up for Jessie's newsletter!

Printed in the USA
CPSIA information can be obtained
at www.ICGtesting.com
LVHW012111260823
756285LV00069B/790